*nightmare
of the embryos*

MARIELLA MEHR

nightmare of the embryos

selected short writings

*translated from the German
by Caroline Froh*

a new directions paperbook original

Copyright © 2026 by Christian Mehr
Copyright © 2026 by Limmat Verlag, Zurich, Switzerland
Copyright © 2026 by Caroline Froh

Texts from the unpublished prose manuscripts of Mariella Mehr,
reproduced by permission of the Swiss Literary Archives (SLA),
Bern (A-1-g-01, A-1-g-02, A-1-g-03, A-1-g-18)

All rights reserved.
Except for brief passages quoted in a newspaper, magazine, radio, television,
or website review, no part of this book may be reproduced in any form
or by any means, electronic or mechanical, including photocopying
and recording, or by any information storage and retrieval system,
or be used to train generative artificial intelligence (AI) technologies
or develop machine-learning language models,
without permission in writing from the Publisher

The Publisher is grateful to the Swiss Arts Council Pro Helvetia
for their generous translation subvention.

swiss arts council
prohelvetia

Manufactured in the United States of America
First published as New Directions Paperbook NDP1656 in 2026

Library of Congress Cataloging-in-Publication Data
Names: Mehr, Mariella, 1947-2022 author | Froh, Caroline translator
Title: Nightmare of the embryos / Mariella Mehr ;
translated from the German by Caroline Froh.
Other titles: Widerworte. English
Description: New York : New Directions Publishing Corporation, 2026. |
Identifiers: LCCN 2025049743 | ISBN 9780811239738 paperback | ISBN
9780811239745 ebook
Subjects: LCGFT: Short stories | Fiction
Classification: LCC PT2673.E43 W5413 2026
LC record available at https://lccn.loc.gov/2025049743

10 9 8 7 6 5 4 3 2 1

New Directions Books are published for James Laughlin
by New Directions Publishing Corporation
80 Eighth Avenue, New York

contents

Memories 3

When Chestnut Blossoms Grew into Your Bedroom . . . 5

Homeland in the Word 8

The Tree 10

We Have Opinions 12

"Did You Know He Wanted a Sin He Had to a Very Grave Mortal Sin" 14

Nightmare of the Embryos 18

On the Aversion to Sensuality in Clay-Pigeon Shooting, or On the Pleasure the Hawk Takes in Killing the Hen   24

Island Body, or The Beach Grass's Failed Attempt to Defeat the North Wind's Laughter 32

A Severed Finger, or The Arrival of the Whale after Sunday Mass 39

Italian Migrant Workers Are Doing Construction Next Door 44

Imparting Wordless, Empty Spaciousness 46

I Would Like to Leave this Borderless White Undescribed 48

It Is Screaming Again 50

The Cell	52
Came Down to the Valley, Leaving Now	54
The Souls of My Sisters and Brothers Are Singing in My Dreams	57
Joseph Sketch	64
Always the Same	66
Snow-Sister	69
The Checkerboard Woman	72
What Do They Accuse Us of?	75
Böcklin on Monte Generoso	77
Eyes	78
Holzpferdchen's Journey	83
Dorian Dreamed	87
Afterword by Caroline Froh	95

nightmare of the embryos

memories

Memories begin with a child's first dreams, they are playthings. You surround yourself with them, lock yourself in. I always dreamt of big, strong women with really round bellies. I thought about the warmth in those bellies. Sometimes I was happily inside them. I built houses around these dreams; they looked just like pregnant women's bellies. Round, soft, and so very warm.

Then the houses grew old. Cracks collected in the walls. The walls crumbled, and with them my dreams—crumbled into silly little pieces.

Nowadays I sit in bars, and sometimes I come across one of these pieces again. In a stranger's face. In the movement of a full, round body. And then I drink—and dreams are there again, not as intense anymore, but still, I would like to build houses around them.

Once, someone wanted to build a house around me on a cold, wintry railroad platform. We couldn't get the trains to stop. Her train always headed west. Houses like that are usually never finished. Longing screams wounds into her voice.

I sit in bars, I drink, memory swims around in glasses, wanting to be free. There's no value in eternity. There are thoughts about death. There is the possibility of death. There is me, and there are the glasses in which memory swims and wishes to set itself free. Now, more and more, I drink too much, and then the memories grow sad.

Sometimes I can find my way to a dream piece without

alcohol, which catches me off guard. You were one of those dream pieces, I wanted to crawl inside of you; there's no value in eternity. I wanted to build a house around you. The important houses are never built. Once, someone wanted to build a house around me. That memory is a hundred years old. Will our feelings fossilize? Like back then? Will they fossilize over us, over you? I draw circles around our tendernesses in spite of it all. There are no houses anymore, only circles.

I will draw and draw until they stay empty. Until their roundness turns to stone, too. Maybe then the possibility of death will become a happy possibility. Maybe then death will bring back the reality held in every childhood dream. Back then, there were women with big, round bellies. And I dreamt of their warmth.

when chestnut blossoms grew into your bedroom

Laughter is a bright wall around us. A ceremony of drunken greetings over at the next table, the noise of belonging together. Hanging overhead, whiffs of cool oil and hungry desire—rosy, edged in black. Housewife faces, student faces, plump partisan mouths, little-girl faces, intellectuals, sensitives—but mostly men. The Weavers, you say, was always a waiting room. The barman carries bad wine from table to table. You have your I-am-strong-on-my-own face on. The noise around us makes your body narrow and fragile, I dream you close to me. The beer sits untouched in our glasses. I feel my way along the edges of our wall, cautiously, my world strange inside of yours. My glass house shatters.

Avanti Popolo bellowed in the background. Frowning shop teacher's face behind the bar. Mouse-gray severity. The sounds come from deep down. Words, chanted, repeated, party slogans, an altar consecrating senselessness, and behind you a piercing green landscape framed in gold. I first came to know this green twenty years ago, in the color of a coat. Back then, the children called me Frog. I wanted to be beautiful. Other girls wore pink bows in their hair. I had a bowl cut—money issues. And with that came the poisonous green coat. *Einen Schnaps* please, Miss, I don't want this green. It's almost midnight, spirit of fatherland in the room. When-the-morning-skies-go-red-etc. People of the taverns, rise up against closing time. Five more minutes for loneliness. A rush of languages, labor-speak, laughter-speak, joke-speak, hunting-speak, manwoman-speak, poison green, is framed in gold. Collecting glances, I'll record them in my planner … maybe another time. And touches, so tidy in their aluminum foil, refrigerator-ready. At home I have an air conditioner, at home you have an air conditioner, at home he she it has an …

We pay together, retrieve our jackets together, open doors, a round of weary adieus, we step under the arbor together, leaving behind the laughter, jumping over the wall, silence. Every house is gray. There it is again, the quiet trembling, butterfly wings of my homesickness. Hey, you left your I-am-strong-on-my-own face behind. They're going to clear it away with all the glasses and bottles.

They play family behind the windows. Father lays on top of mother, children are sleeping in the next room, wrapped up skyblue with rosy cheeks. The doll from the Jelmoli department store. Midnight. The long march of asocials; we are not a family.

I say hello to the girl on the corner. Washed-out eyeblue, her mouth a bloodred cave. Borderless face, an attic smell and cheap cologne in her artificial hair.

In The Säbel, a pimp drinks himself to death. Sleep, my little prince, in your smoky room. A man with a broad farmer's face plays the little prince's melody on his fiddle. Tenderness hangs naked in the corner of his mouth. One more *Kaffelutz* so I don't have to see your eyes. I want to explain everything on your front stoop. One more *Kaffelutz*, another last call waits with dangling wings. The fat server hands out fatherly farewell smiles. Through the smoke, the little prince sleeps with hospital eyes. Then the dead pimp comes slurring back to life. Lisa, show your attic face under the streetlamp. Bare your borderlessness as the train of pitiful masculinity shuffles past your silver-stockinged legs. Even the moon has abandoned us.

Ever-grayer sandstone, the worn handle of your front door. Chestnut blossoms, you say, are growing through your bedroom window. Give me my island back, before I leave you. Maybe I'll explain it all to you tomorrow.

homeland in the word

My uncle, Alois the Basketmaker, was a gifted storyteller. He delighted bar-goers with his arsenal of stories and histories over a glass of wine or *Kafifertig*, and imparted wit and wisdoms to his friends and kin on nights spent around the campfire. Wit and wisdoms that, while they didn't quite explain the hard life of a Traveler, still made it easier to endure, and transformed these hours around the fire into something magical. When Alois the Basketmaker developed cancer, he had to be admitted to the district hospital. It was as if Travelers didn't have enough stones thrown in their path while they were living (which usually made for a painful stumble); they couldn't even make their way unscathed down the loneliest path of all, the one leading to their death. That was the end of the stories and transcendent campfires, the end of those beers, of wine and *Kafifertigs*. Alois went mute, wilted in his white hospital bed. His personal maxim: *Alles weiss der Aloweis*,* which was how each of his stories began and ended, and had lost its meaning in those gray hospital hallways, for this place couldn't offer any lessons on dying joyfully, not for my uncle, who already knew what it meant to live joyfully. The place where stories are told, said my uncle, that's our homeland. A rainbow, he said, that connects us to everyone and everything. But then my uncle wrested one more story from life—he split, left through the back

---

* "Alowise knows everything." —Tr.

door in nothing but a hospital gown and an old coat, which in better days had been his protection from the cold, back when he overnighted in straw huts. He split, *vertschanet*, as Travelers say; he sought out the place that meant the most to him, the Mellinger forest, in order to die there, at the forest's edge. Not alone, no, for at that time there was at the edge of the forest a little house, and in this house lived an old woman, his Maja, as he called this friend. One of the women who listened to his stories, who gave him bread and cheese in thanks, on occasion with a slice of ham, or a jacket left behind by her late husband. It was to Maja that Alois ran off in order to tell his final story, the story of his death. He died peacefully, Maja assured us later, a relief, as people say. He was taken in by the Word.

the tree

It was the biggest and came from Denmark. We don't have that kind of green here. Even its needles were longer. And anyway. I had to have it. Because it was the biggest.

"You must have an entire marketplace or train station at your house," remarked the person who sold it to me, and I paid cash.

The tree was monstrous, which complicated its transport. But then came the three, each one a sign complete with two legs and two hands, gesturing wildly toward my tree.

"Hello," I said, "there you are. This tree needs to make it by Christmas. And listen, you scruffy little crusaders, rest your cause against the wall for now, it's not the last you're going to see of it."

They were full of complaints as they pulled; the signs they'd been carrying hadn't elicited half as much noise. They started to sweat, and then we were there. The entryway was too narrow, but it was made of glass, which we broke for the good cause.

"Six more flights," I said, "nothing's too high for Christmas." But the three let the tree fall, and then they disappeared. I didn't have to sit on my tree for long. Another man came and said: "This is going to cost you."

"As it should," I said. "What else do you think Christmas is for?"

The man left. And I was left to ponder how best to proceed with this story, because it seemed to be driving itself. The elevator opened without a sound, and the janitor said,

"Stormy weather out there ..." It was the first time either of us had said a word to the other.

"Something different for a change, don't you agree?"

"And how exactly do you see this working out?"

"It's going to be splendid," I said.

"It needs to go," he said.

"Of course it does, but how?"

"Chop it up," he said.

But then the man stumbled and nicked himself on the glass. "This won't do," I said and pulled the fire alarm. It didn't take long.

"Where's the fire?" the firemen asked.

"At my place," I said.

"And the blood?"

"One thing at a time," I said.

And that's how the tree made it to the sixth floor, and how the doors came off their hinges. "Keep going," I said. "I'm sure you can see this tree isn't fit for a room. Take it out to the balcony." So there it stood, finally, two stories tall. I sat down.

"This is going too far," someone shouted from the window above me.

"We all overdo it once in a while," I said.

"But this is over the top!" he screamed.

"Indeed," I said.

"And what am I supposed to do about this?!"

"Do whatever you want."

"I'm going to saw it down," he threatened.

"You can't do that."

"Just you watch," he cried.

"Everything in moderation," I warned.

And with that he fell out of his window. Christmas could finally come.

we have opinions

We have opinions. We are allowed to have them and we do, they are preconceived, imposed, conformist, nitpicky, generous, different—it's just that they aren't our own.

I offer an opinion again ... you, you, you, he, she, it, I, you, he, she, it ... and now we're speaking to one another. Inside of opinions, others. I lean against the concrete wall. The stars are sputtering bane and bile, violent night, the last of the truck drivers are still out in the streets, yawning, cursing, their caps pushed back on their heads, I hear the howling of unloved dogs, the moonlessness is above me. I know people are sleeping on the other side of the windows, their dreams sprawl out inside their rooms, restless, dark, unwieldy, smoldering.

The sound of old Tomi shuffling across the gravel. Now that he's older, he says, sleep slips away from him at night. So Tomi wanders past the howling dogs, past the caravans, the high-wheeled old wooden wagons and the modern, metal ones. Radio Beromünster rings in the dawn ... This is how you ration time. Nights, too. We meet: Tomi—from whom sleep is running away, giggling with glee—and I, with the memory of loveless conversations below my heart, and my belly burning from one last violent touch.

A conversation, opinions, different opinions, pain from stabbing one another, deliberately, intentionally, and meanwhile hate licks the blood from the knife, satisfied; we have opinioned ourselves out.

Nights, Tomi says, he longs for the forests, where screech owls sound the death knell with their mournful call. Some still believe in that. Tomi's father, at least, died shortly after the call. Afterward, his caravan was set on fire and there were three days of celebration. A rollicking celebration with homemade schnapps and little elderberry cakes, because it was spring. That's where Tomi wants to go—and thinks back on his seventy-four years.

"did you know he wanted a sin he had to a very grave mortal sin"

When one writes very quietly, writes themselves into the quiet, writes and writes into the long nights of questioning with a muted mouth, becoming quieter, quieter still. And there's sorrow and perhaps the fear of failing to let the muted mouth go silently into the night, into the long nights of doubt, into those timeless nights with only this scent of fall in their words, words that experience life as inescapable loss, as a chain of hardship and fear and rage and violence and the animal part of the soul, which wants to break out and flail around, sparing no one, itself least of all, since there aren't images for this, there are no signposts, no dams against the terror and hardship and fear and rage and violence. Words, breakable like children's bodies; no hand in reach where they'd be well placed, secure, no hand in reach to protect their delicate clarity. A text, its word choice transparent, its language a metaphor for the failure of that language—art language, as my friend A. S. called it—but the art of this text doesn't lie in what is said, no, it lies more so in what is left unspoken, the secrets between sentences, a transparent secrecy as thread-fine as the words themselves: unity that gives even someone like me the time to explore the secret within the realm of my own experience.

And so I sit down, read. In order to stand right back up again, and pace, pace back and forth, in time with the text, its music. In order not to drown in the secrecy between the lines, which is also mine—woman or not. Woman or not, back and forth, I repeat this to see whether there is something there that extends beyond the division of man and woman, something to do with fists, perhaps, your own.

Appeasing the unruly rhythm of the text. What a thing to say, when it causes your heart and hands to bleed, these hands—this pressing shut, this holding fast to hate and love, interwoven and thereby canceled out, yes, a new dimension, not yet considered by the likes of us; I think: this is the new.

I am at your tender throat, incarnate, with my hands, in the name of the Father, the Mother, and everyone else with pain like this, foreverandeveramen. I am at your throat. Let no one tell me your throat isn't a real place. Homecoming through death, which, once the card is dealt, releases me from my placelessness. Something resembling thankfulness in the silence. This comes after.

When I finally carried the text out of the house. Carried it to the Saint Lawrence chapel (I often say there's too much to see there: the Rhine, the Rhine valley, the Piz Beverin mountain, the ash groves, ruins of castles whose names I can never remember, which are said to have housed Jenatsch,* at least temporarily, that uncouth hero, and even the ashes, these wild-growing, wall-jumping, indecent, unmanageable beings). I carried it to the chapel as a gift, left it surrounded by the ashes and the sacred that's said to have surrounded Lawrence; a deer screamed. I have a habit of bringing texts to Lawrence, the ones I can't understand and others so near

---

* Georg Jenatsch (1596–1639) was a Swiss political and military hero during the Thirty Years' War. —Tr.

to me I can hardly stand their nearness. And so I heard a cry and I read "The Lost Story"*—so near to me I can hardly stand its nearness—leaning against the wall, bare feet in the blooming lousewort, meadow sage, lady's mantle, wild thyme; and this deer screamed, and all I could make of this was that it had simply screamed, that this soft hill, overgrown with herbs, is fond of eliciting cries, far removed from any sort of zoological explanation, simple as that. Pink clouds adorned Piz Berevin like cotton candy—and indeed why should it appear any other way, when deer scream and lousewort sprawls across the bare feet of someone like me—my mouth felt sticky.

Near Lawrence, happiest of all the martyrs, near this man who had himself roasted alive. Almost a fakir, a legend like that. As a child I tried to imagine being there, standing next to him, this man who lay on the gridiron and died. Was he on his stomach, facing the refracted eyes of the earth and glowing embers burning their death marks into his flesh? Or on his back, eyes lost in the starry sky? Today, mindful of the most recent wars, mindful of all the atrocities committed, this happy fantasy has lost its charm, death has lost its innocence, pain its magnitude, irreversible. But here, on the Lawrence hill, at the foot of the Lawrence chapel, the

---

* This piece is in many ways a direct response to "Die Verlorene Geschgichte" (The lost story) by Otto F. Walter. In the story, a twenty-eight-year old unemployed ironworker named Polo Ferro (whose name literally translates to "Iron Pole" or "Iron Stake") kills his girlfriend, a Thai woman named "Thai," at a picnic in a fit of passion. Walter's story explores the sudden shift from gentleness to brutality and love to violence, along with language and speechlessness. It also recounts xenophobic incidents that occurred in Switzerland during the years leading up to the story's publication in 1993. —Tr.

deer cries out, and I read that somewhere someone named Polo Ferro lived, and if I trace his name back to the cradle, he would have to be called "he-who-was-purified-in-iron" or "he-who-was-transformed-in-iron." I read toward sin, toward "very grave sin," toward "mortal sin." For someone like me, brought up Catholic, mortal sin has remained the secret par excellence, a pagan custom, delicious in its darkness and all the human incomprehension that surrounds it. Sin keeps doubt in line and gives the act the tenderness it deserves. The act as insurgent against privilege, set to die in the rot of reason. Let us follow the cry of the deer, the metamorphoses are manifold, the risk of your life passing you by is too great.

The pink clouds have released Piz Beverin. Snow glitters cold and blue at its peak. The deer can no longer be heard. Thai is dead. She took the very grave sin, the mortal sin, away with her as sustenance for the journey. Look at the grass and the mother, look at the wild thyme, the meadow sage, and lousewort sprawling across bare feet.

Laughing Lawrence.

He is dead, blown away by another's pain. What a fallacy, life: an abominable accident. Here, someone captured him, did a good job of it, proved their courage.

nightmare of the embryos

It was always about that. The search for a lost land. Love. This fucked-up youth, always exploited, betrayed, bribed, lost. Lies, sadism, the stronger ones' malicious laughter. Love, useless pastime, it was bad enough that the children at the home had to be fed. During the day they were rough, in their boundless fury they mutilated what little was still human.

Night then—we were rolled up together like embryos in strange sheets—was another world. Dormitories, embryos in beds, craving a womb. Blue nightlight (the eye of Justice, judging), each exhale a meager tenderness for the foreign embryo beside you. Night: groping hands in the darkness, mothlike thoughts, longing dreamed into an inhuman emptiness, screaming children's prayers, ice cream, icebergs, unconsciousness. Night: children's great no-man's-land. We were also worthy of love. But we didn't want to live. Night: the matron's metallic voice, too. We waited, trembling, for her call, and each embryo crept back into their own unfamiliar bed. Each child was an only child—we were not a family!

The nights in these rooms, those cursed nights of unwanted children.

Luzern 1950. A children's home at the edge of the forest. It had its own park, henhouse, Sisters of the Seraphic Love Mission. The steps at the front of the house were a child's Matterhorn, gigantic in my memory, unclimbable. Don't step down into the street of the people, where there are children and playground balls, parents and strong boys. Don't step down, danger lurks at the bottom. A woman stood there who had come for a pretty child. She stood there, noisy, and waved at me behind my invisible cage, waved with red fingers, my mother, who wanted a pretty child and reeked of alcohol. It looked as if laughter had slipped to the corners of her mouth and hung there in a cold grin. She wanted a doll child, a play child. I was ugly and squinted. One of the sisters' hands clasped my arm, raised it high. And so I waved, too, with broken-winged fingers, I waved at my mother, who always celebrated Christmas without me, who stood there at the bottom of the steps, without tenderness.

December 1951. St. Nicholas, you good man, they sang, because he loved the well-behaved children, they clung to his red, quilted robe and fingered his beard. They all laughed. I was a bed wetter, I was ugly and squinted. I broke the other children's toys, bombed their sandcastles, and tortured the hens in their henhouse. I stole. And because of this I spent Christmas Eve in a well-sewn gunnysack "outside in the cold." The love of the holy man was reserved for the others, the "dry ones," the "upright ones." I listened to the muffled cries of joy of the two hundred children in the decorated hall. I dreamt of mandarin oranges and was filled with hate. Grown-up footsteps. They stopped in front of my sack, this lumpy brown sack with the child trapped inside. In the great room, they had vanilla pudding and syrup to celebrate. I was a bed wetter and squinted, and they called my mother a drunken slut. She never came back. They called it alcoholic psychosis and locked her in a mental hospital. It sounded less unseemly, alcoholic psychosis. I had a sick mother now.

Altendorf 1953. I listened to his dry sobs as he beat me. Anyone who loves their child—even a foster child—shows it by beating them as they scream from beneath the leather belt. He lost two fingers in the factory's sheet-metal cutter, came back from America with the black lung. I apologized to him for my existence. A tall, skinny woman laughed. I stole a pair of skis in revenge. They're from the Christkind, I said, and believed it. Because of this, the psychiatrist called me a compulsive liar.

The skinny woman was a seamstress. In my free time, I watched her clients as they tried on her clothes. I sat on the red plush sofa and watched the naked women with their jiggling breasts and folds of fat around their bellies. They stood there in their pink slips and sweaty faces. They fixed their leering eyes on me—me, who was really a girl. I hid my eyes at the level of the table that stood between us. Then I stole coins from their bags, which they usually left in the kitchen. They called me little hussy, and my foster father hit me, crying as he did so. I was the foundling of the village.

Hagendorn 1955. The ambulance drove up. Terrifying men climbed out and took the girl away with them. The girl whose arms had held me close, night after night, tender and childlike and desperate. She lay on a stretcher, one of her arms missing. She'd been pushed under a truck. They had laughed at us, we were depraved youth. They laughed and picked her off the stone floor of the bathroom where we lay, naked; the face of the merciful sister from the Sacred Heart and the broken bamboo were above us. The girl didn't cry, she didn't scream. She just stared straight ahead, hate in her eyes, and on her a face a look that knew nothing of childhood. Above her and me the sister with the blue lips. Heart problems, someone explained to me later—and—we had killed her. The guilt stayed with us both. I was small and couldn't feel anything. The men carried the armless girl away. The arm lay under the truck, and we didn't have the first clue what to do with it.

Menzingen 1956. There were no conclusions to be drawn. This was as much a home as any other, not any better, the dormitories were just the same. Only, the fact of my being a girl became heavier, became something to be recorded. They hit differently now and the walls grew higher, the invisible cage more obvious, uglier. To be a girl was an added sentence. They taught me to direct hate toward my own body, which was dirty, full of filthy desires. They struck my body in cold sewing rooms, in dark hallways, at dinner tables, in the cellar. They called me Mario there and gave me a blue felt cap. I stayed Mario for years afterward; later I bought myself red men's shirts.

Altstätten 1957. Shards of glass. The Sisters of the Good Shepherd, penitents before the Lord. Mournful chorales during Sunday worship. It was cool in the church, all the girls in blue and white. It was cool. The sun shone outside on the walls topped with the shards of glass and barbed wire. Larkspur in the garden. At the edge of the wall a nettle field and cigarette butts.

Inside these walls the sisters beat us as a warning, with penitent faces, with whacking hands. They cried out the name of Christ, and we laughed. Our hearts had long been hardened against beatings and Christ. The sisters wore metal hearts on their chest and an image of Christ with his thorny crown, the suffering Jesus. He smiled benignly at our naked backs. He smiled through the hard eyes of the nuns, he smiled at the mournful singing in the dark church, he smiled over our screaming, he smiled and pointed his finger at our girls' friendships in warning. He smiled. At night I climbed over the walls with shards of glass and barbed wire. I broke my leg, looked for the street, and he smiled. He smiled in the space between the car driver and myself, over the hand on my knees, he smiled past my fear, past the disheveled bed, past the man's hands and onto the flabby grin. Later the man with the hands gave me a train ticket to Zürich. There I ate blue bird-berries out of a stranger's garden. My stomach was a patch of nettles. I screamed in pain. He smiled still, the suffering Jesus.

St. Gallen 1958. The carnival was in town, bright lights. Music and cotton candy. I didn't know what to do with my freedom, where to begin. I'd left my personal belongings at the home: a journal and cut-out pictures of saints. The girls sang sad seafaring songs. Someone was playing the harmonica. That's why, hours later, I stood in the middle of the city in a blue skirt and a blue windbreaker. I had a hole in my sock. My shoe rubbed against my skin. It was cold. People played family behind the windows.

Zürich 1958. St. Josefsheim. Christ smiled here, too. A smug smile, only for families, rounded-out ones, the children with the innocent eyes. I was now some kind of monster. This youth, this intelligence, they said, and: Surely it wasn't all that terrible. In the future, I'd have to ... There is no future for embryos, for unwanted children. And their Christ smiled later as uniformed men frisked my body, rifled through my bags, and found a Nivea tin and a toothbrush.

Chur 1958. I lay on a white bed. The face of the psychiatrist was above my abdomen, his finger in my hole. Just a very small pain, as Christ smiled. It had to be that way for the report. I bled later. In his report it said: hereditarily polluted, difficult to educate. During freetime, the psychiatrist played chess with me, grabbed at my little boy's body with his eyes, he promised to help me.

Luzern 1959. Another edge of a forest. You could run away in there. The forest was fenced in. They knew that I'd turn back. They knew and laughed. After every escape they stuck me in the bathroom, warmed my stomach with leftover dinner. I was their most interesting animal, they could pet and hit me.

My mother wrote from her institution. She wrote a poem about free, open nature. About the biggest animal in the forest, the big, strong animal, and lots of little people. Weeks after that, she sent me sewing supplies, and I forgot about the animal and the poem. I dreamt later of a wolf and many laughing, screaming, sneering people. The wolf tore me apart, and spared only a dress. A blue and white, very very short one.

Zug 1961. Nietzsche under the covers and Sartre, unsatisfactory in German. We smelled most of the time of turpentine and cigarettes. I ate my friend's food package. She watched me as I ate, I ate up thirteen years of hunger, chocolate and sausage. Nights remained dreamless, I didn't scream anymore.

Cham 1962. Apathy is a great mother. Even Christ didn't smile on this indifference anymore.

Les Granges 1963. Monsieur kept teenage girls to pass the time. His wife was ugly and drank.

Chur 1964. There was no doctor anymore. They brought out files about my mother and called her a drunken whore. I didn't suffer anymore. I barely felt the shock. The gray machine with its many wires. Wires that held the body captive and had the power to break bones—and the will. It no longer mattered. I heard other women screaming because of its violence. They screamed and wandered through the rooms with naked faces like sleepwalkers. They ate grape sugar and rocked imaginary children in their arms. I ceased being a child.

Hindelbank 1966. We were also worthy of love, though we didn't want to live. I woke up on a mountain of rubble that should apparently have been called childhood. In my belly grew a new embryo.

on the aversion to sensuality in clay-pigeon shooting, or on the pleasure the hawk takes in killing the hen

Before now, I hang unsheltered (naturally, otherwise they'd
accuse me of the worst schizophrenia; heil the madhouse),
wrapped only in fragile skin,
in position,
in the naked branches of a tree, and I
learn how to fly in the slipstream of the hawk.

Flying low
he circles the roof
in his swoop he grazes
the silver glistening shingles
and red/red delicately feathered heads of the hens
behind the barn with its silver-glinting
shingled roof system recalibration
if the body is a system
maybe a slight correction
to my alpine farm idyll
symmetry or maybe it's
only hunger that drives
him into my territory.

I froze

up in the branches I froze
cuckoo's fruit.

If I can trust the history of the last eighty years, I can assume that, another hundred and fifty years ago, I would have likely been burned at the stake.
I consider it done. Just like

The murder of my mother, though it was an unremarkable heart attack in the end,
a result of her deep-seated distrust
of death, which forced her to continue living.

Also worth mentioning

the murders of my
father my grandfather
my grandmother my aunts
and uncles
the murder of my brother.

He did it, twelve years young, he did it with a bed sheet, with a piss-soaked bed sheet on the flagstones of the St. Josef home, a home for the mentally handicapped, he did it with a piss-soaked bed sheet, snaked the piss-soaked sheet around his neck on the flagstones, after he was forced to stand before the other boys at breakfast.

   He stood in front of them with the wet sheet pressed against his chest as if in a trance, stood before these boys who pounced on him at the nuns' command, pounced on him jeering and mocking him, jeering and mocking this boy with the submissive shoulders and now chronic trembling in his limbs, his eyes probably closed, struggling to suppress sobs, he stood before them, stood there with the piss-soaked sheet

and did not defend himself this final time.

For my grandfather, it was in a prison cell. He died like a dog, with lungs devoured by tuberculosis. They retrieved his body from the stinking hole days afterward, buried him in a pauper's grave; not even the pigs would touch the rotten meals of those last five days, they said, meaning the days of his agony.

I heard my mother crying out for her father just before she died. A terrible, childlike cry: Father, Father, why have you forsaken me? She didn't know he was dead, had wasted away behind bars, miserably, decades before. She cried out for her father in the voice of a five-year-old, the way she probably cried out back when the lords of Graubünden and their henchmen ripped her from her clan to be "transplanted in healthy soil," code for: workhouses and madhouses.

"Moral imbecility" was what they called her desperate self-defense; her hatred of her tormentors would amount in their reports to "moral degeneracy of a compulsive, unstable, and mentally deficient psychopath."

She never lived a day.

Only ever cried out for her father and her mother in her dreams and pissed and shit the bed in the madhouses and prisons.

When at seventeen and pregnant I cried out for my father and mother in Cell 24 of Hindelbank women's prison, I didn't know that twenty years earlier, in the same prison, in the same "healthy soil," my mother howled for her mother and father and brothers and sisters

and pissed the bed
like my brother and I
fearing that this
would be the rest of our lives.

My mother called it a dog's life, and there were never any flowers in her dreams, and the ones who did it to her never offered the slightest comfort to the ravaged creature she was, no, not the slightest bit, not to her and not to the child in her aching stomach.

And when after the war a world defiled cried out for absolution, for a pure world, and the cowardly silent majority was horror-stricken by the murders committed by the man they themselves had elected, and when the millions of graves overflowing with the uninvited guests of this century caused shame to permeate everything—in our country, after the final bullet meant for traitors had been discharged by a uniformed mob, our tormentors still sat tall in their saddles, the soul eaters and body mutilators continued to feed on the souls of my brothers and sisters, continued to feed on our bodies, unchecked by the anger of left wing -isms and -ists; we weren't worthy of any humanitarian speech or revolutionary thought.

We were easy to overlook: Nobody's Children.

Because we'd never had a voice, just hate-fed hearts and clenched teeth and stunted spirits, always running away from something.

And while my mother's sister—who, thanks to the help of a nun, had been snatched from the Nazis in Strasbourg in the nick of time—sat in the Bellechasse penitentiary (an immigrant with a Swiss passport, barely sixteen), this country boasted of being Europe's fortress against fascism, despite the rejected Jewish refugees and despite the borders closed to persecuted Gypsies and the vaults opened to melted-down victim gold.

But my aunt forgot to tell them why she sat in Bellechasse to begin with, which crimes she'd made herself guilty of in order to scrub jail floors for four years in atonement.

In a psychiatric report she would later be denounced as a moronic, compulsive, and depraved psychopath.

Our jailers' work filled books and libraries. The most shameless of these brown lowlifes earned doctorates and glory off of our bent backs, their disgusting praise of fascist eugenics for the supposed health of the Volk still hangs over our heads. We remain substandard human goods.

"The very best letters ..." and I began this piece as a letter despite missing a salutation, because who really wants to address someone with *dear* or *to the honorable leftists*, or *comrades,* given that these words have long decayed into elitist secret society speak— anyway, "the very best letters are those that are never sent" George Bernard Shaw said, and so I'd like to continue writing as if this were really a kind of letter, as if someone really were sitting there and reading the pain and the rage and helplessness between the lines. Maybe I'll give this someone my diaries to read later, scattered as they are to the four winds, meaning, never ordered according to month or day, since there's always a postscript to tuck in somewhere, and these lines are probably something like that themselves, an addition; maybe writing in whatever form is only an addition of things to which one attaches significance, forgetting that things simply *are* without significance, that it's only in their addition that they acquire it.

To carry forward the unhappy history of my brothers and sisters—and my own—means that my hatred becomes subordinate to my thinking. I am carrying it toward a future where there is at least a possibility our children will find new laughter.

It's easy to laugh when you're facing death, what else can you do. This laughter, in turn, means I'm thinking. Thinking, I took what I knew of their bloodlust and stripped it from their bones, so to speak, then waited for it to poison me.

Nothing happened. Just a shock when I discovered the banality of what I once mistook for greatness, absolute greatness, heroic courage in the face of evil. I recognized the reality of the banal: an ambitionless, bourgeois, disgusting, slimy narrow-mindedness that failed to derive any pleasure from true evil; it was never capable—mindless, the way it was celebrated—of reckoning with the consequences of its actions.

The hawk's happiness
in its plunge

toward earth its beak blows
shred the slender neck
red blood the golden throat
feathers color the childlike
down in deathlight shining
the smile of the hen friendship
the smile of the hawk sweet
the warmth of torn
flesh.

When they maimed our women's bodies, castrated our men, they did so without pleasure, without innocence, without the happiness of those who are truly evil. It was their own humiliating impotence, their genitalia-fixated phobias that cried out for relief, for some sort of balance, because their leprous cocks had no healing caves to soothe them, their bodies, born blind, demanded pedestals, their greed was lacking no matter the size, boundless only in its cowardice.

Their heaven remained a stinking latrine, fly-swarmed and filled with the rotting residue of their obscene fantasies. They lacked that blessed panic which alone enables conscious destruction, that glorious fear that unites victim and perpetrator in the end:

We became victims, because we feared them.

And it is not
the pure feces
of a holy obscenity's expenditure
leavened with the yeast
of every lustful thought

of the hawk's body
it is not this fully-ripened form
no it is the stinking
excretion of an anus no sun
has ever touched and
pitiful it remains
in pain, not in functional
satisfaction, not the
hawk's laughter.

He was never meant to be a metaphor
he ripped the livers from the defenseless
right out of their gold-plumed bodies and
it was hardly pleasure when his
mighty wings brushed the curious Earth
I heard the air hold its breath
afterward the silence became
a wholly joyful requiem.

According to bourgeois standards of utility, we amount to an unproductive expenditure of the most beautiful uselessness. This is our value.

island body, or the beach grass's failed attempt to defeat the north wind's laughter

(for W.)

the lonely beach grass tried with songs that the sand dunes had sung to him before this dream, soft, gentle hill melodies. before this dream they brought sea buckthorn and wild roses into bloom and made the black gulls' screaming temporarily fall silent. a failed attempt to remember the colors of his former homeland.

In the time before, he gave her a knife. She kept it in her left pocket. This is also where she liked to hide her left hand, usually balled into a fist. In her right pocket, her right hand was usually clutching a small, stuffed bear or a smooth, polished pebble. She selected her pocket contents according to how they felt inside her hand. Snail shells and mussels were just as suitable as pebbles or plush bears. String felt nice too, or larger, dried-out breadcrumbs, which offered the hands something like resistance.

    She called the little leather pouch around her neck "the suitcase." Inside were two poems that W. had written to her in the time before, a blue glass bead, some pills for her nerves, a piece of petrified knife handle from the pile-dwelling period, a one-centime coin, a violet stone from the ochre caves of Roussillon, and occasionally a piece of trash, which, like everything else, she only attributed a ritual remembered significance to and therefore kept for months until it became unusable.

I sat with my back to the north wind and protected the lonely beach grass with my body. I ran new hands along the glossy, silver surface of its coarse stalks. The sea sang its ebb song and an oystercatcher followed that maternal rhythm, then silently soared into the air. Today I would learn to stop the beach grass from freezing. Today I would learn the cry of the gulls.

In her daydreams, she often tried to capture the warmth that collected in the leaves of trees. She lived in tree houses, but generously gave them away as soon as a human offered themselves as a temporary dwelling. There seemed to be some primal urge that compelled her to inhabit everything, be it the gentle curve of a river, the constellation of the Great Bear (this seemed particularly fateful to her), a person's skin, the inside of a mountain. She rarely inhabited herself, remaining instead a stranger, a wanderer, a vagabond. Her being-human often took her by surprise, and felt like something that did not belong to her. In those moments she would try desperately to remember her contours, looking for a beginning and ending to her self, for a clear and analyzable index of her physicality, for the road at the end of which she expected to be whole. Otherwise, she sometimes experienced herself in pieces.

what was the condition of his former roots?
    the beach grass's memories became increasingly sparse, colorless, soundless. he found himself on an iceberg and heard the laughter of the north wind. it was white and merciless.

I began to make myself at home in my new island body. With new hands I still protected the lonely, dreaming beach grass. Wings grew timidly on me, though I waited patiently. Over on the neighboring island, new-time made final preparations to give a sister peace.

She had her mother's heavy eyelids over narrow, mouse-gray eyes. Her breathing sounded asthmatic, like it was being pressed out between two invisible walls, and her long face looked squeezed, as though it couldn't fit properly anywhere. Around her slightly sullen, youthful mouth, a few fine lines that widened and deepened as they ran down to a weak, shapeless chin. Her hair hung in front of her face, and single, sun-bleached strands stuck to her oily cheeks. Her eyes were set at uneven depths in their sockets. Above the bridge of her nose, almost precisely in the center of two finely-drawn eyebrows, there cowered, so to speak, a red birthmark. She was still a child when her mother told her the mark would burst open and begin to bleed with every lie she told. And so she lied secretly her whole life. Whenever she did, she took care to cover the mark with her left hand because, as she had learned from an early age, the left hand was the evil one anyway. It was best used to wipe your bottom, and good people greeted other good people with their right.

When she was young, she never did get along with the scouts. They greeted people with their left hand.

She had the smell typical of a frightened person. She felt fear somewhere in the middle of her body as a ravenous animal, parasite-like, a demanding twin that gobbled up her lentil dish, and thus the energies that struggled to keep her alive.

She felt this fear even now on her island, even though she knew that the small amount of energy still available was hardly substantial for hungry animals. She trudged through the central dunes to the island's eastern beach. A strange thought made her laugh dryly. It would read: "Cause of death not yet determined," and note that the dead woman was a foreigner, probably from the south.

with cutting laughter, the north wind brought him illusions of all that had happened before this dream. the surf on his island's eastern shore, and gentle nighttime exhalations of the stunted pine trees that once feebly protected his roots. the cold became space and space became ice and white became all of time. he would fall into this white, something that never was, he would never again know the island as it had been before this dream. the beach grass shivered in the cold.

Farther down the beach began the other journey of the washed-up flotsam: mussels, crabs, little jellyfish, beetles, scattered fish. The stranded creatures died noiselessly, without distress, without questions, completely unquestioning, the way life is lived far from human consequence.

So this, then, is the texture of escape. She trudged farther toward the beach. Her steps slowed when she heard melodies that she had listened to before, with other ears, with W. It was the slow movement from a piano concerto, whose composer she could no longer recall. She thought of his storm-mouth, which, laughing, had destroyed her home. She would have to break the thread, the silver cord connecting her to him. More of a levelheaded resolution than a desperate thought. To her, the time yet to be lived was a kind of rinse water, and she was a pupfish who still had to live through it. A pupfish perhaps because this fish appeared to her the most human, and by choosing it she believed she could feel some of its innate malleability. When she was finished, dying would no longer be in the foreground, nor death—instead, the severing of this silver cord. There was no question about the operation's legitimacy. The whole thing seemed reasonable enough, save for a few disturbing thoughts that had stayed behind. Who would brush the hair out of his eyes? Although there was no time left to smile, she did, almost tenderly, when she remembered his youthful face and his eyes, which shone like polished chestnuts. Becoming-human, she thought, happens only rarely. She had missed her own opportunity, but he still had his before him. She no longer felt any anger she could save herself with. She thought of a sentence she had written to him in the time before: "If we only had dreams, dreams to give each other like flowers, but all that grows beneath our silent hands are tears."

he dreamt he died without having been born. he dreamt he awoke unable to remember any story that could have told him about his earlier, plant existence. he found himself once again a repository of unfamiliar stories. and laughter inthewind, inthewind. his identity, extinguished in this terrible white. he no longer remembered an island, it was nobody's place.

I dreamt they stole my sex. I awoke and did not recognize myself. I searched for my name, the length of my body over, I searched for my story, but found only the names and stories of others. I felt around my space for anything familiar but could find nothing that belonged to me, because I did not know who I was. I was called Sirokurtwalterchristopherrichardmaxreto ... my identity, extinguished in this terrible white.

Now and then materialized hints of womens' names, in a kind of halting recognition, if only briefly, like stars in the mist, and dark blue was the night that surrounded them.

An unbearable timelessness seemed to be flowing through me, a sea of nothingness where I had once been. I no longer inhabited my self; astonishment followed fear and panic. I was tempted to scream but abandoned the thought, because I couldn't be sure whether it would be me screaming or "her." My surroundings began to dissolve and pushed their way into another time that only knew circles. Floating, pale pink circles, seeking, colliding, dancing in and out of one another until all that was left was a soft, soothing red, like wine, which I had enjoyed drinking in the time before. I wandered through this strange interval, my head now light with namelessness, released from others' stories, though I did not possess my own name, or my own story. I continued to wander, floating, like the circles, until my center came to understand its own rhythm, and follow it. Tentative at first, and blind, afraid, then happier.

Faces appeared, fathers, millions of fathers. Their eyes contained the hardness of sharpened steel, their lips the frigid blue of ice. They pushed past me and I screamed, and I knew suddenly that it was me screaming. I screamed for the terrible timelessness occupying my body, this sea of nothingness my energy had been victim to for years, decades, centuries, millenia. I screamed and I became the scream, until something new grazed my consciousness.

A mussel, purple like the stone from the Roussillon cliffs, violet rings spiraling around its matte shell, its insides deep yellow and glowing, as if it were inhabited by the moon. I studied the mussel in amazement, the spiral pattern vibrating ever so slightly. Skin dissolved from flesh until I, naked now and unprotected, began the process of forgetting every conceivable human form. My consciousness drew closer to the mussel's until I understood and absorbed it to be a primordial form. The spiral solidified into a fine net that wrapped itself around me until I too could be absorbed into this ancient pattern, become part of this originality, which was feminine and earth. I became a part, and at the same time whole. I awoke from a long nightmare of false conditioning, misunderstanding, the performative and artificial. Somewhere within me opened a singular eye. My sense of the golden iris surpassed my knowledge of it. With this eye I could see for the briefest moment into the depths of names I had been looking for: Eurynome, Isis, Gaia, Sarasvati, Anahita, Lakshmi, Kali. I forgot human speech and began to hum, as I had tried to do in the time before, in the humming caves of Malta. It was the OM of the earth, subordinate to none of the fathers. The OM of the earth in whose primal caves lived those who unified life with the living. It was the original sound of all life. I wept and was. In this beingness I found my way back to you again, I found your face and looked upon it without fear.

She gave him this vision again, one final time, as she stroked his hair gratefully, with a tender smile. She laid down and knew that it was time to climb into the depths, into her own depths. She thought without regret about how in her uneventful life there would have been only this single event. She would have died "of unknown causes." No one would understand that death could never be as absurd as her life had been. For what could be more absurd than suffering for the one she loved?

A long distance away, the companion waited—still powerful, even as she grieved. She lay down beside a cluster of lonely beach grass and waited. The stone from Roussillon felt pleasing in her hand.

a severed finger, or the arrival of the whale after sunday mass

The Pfäffikon train station in the canton of Schwyz is a small station. When Mr. Kälin signaled green to continue the journey, the platform and shelter were already empty, as if the arriving passengers, blinded by the unfiltered light, had immediately sought refuge and fled like mice into the nearest cracks and holes. When it rained, the station emptied out more slowly, because then people were opening umbrellas or pulling hats over ears before the group continued what little was left of their journey on foot. For most, the destination was the Verwo factory across from the station. You could pick out the factory workers by their heavy gait, their sleep-hooded eyes, and their skin, which shimmered a colorless gray like the umbrellas opened in the rain.

Whenever the factory workers went to work, they seemed to have just gotten out of bed, because they worked shifts and only slept when it suited their boss. They smelled of metal, machine oil, and cigarette butts, and metal dust blackened their pores. That's why their skin shimmered gray even on Sundays, because you couldn't wash it off or scrub it clean; you couldn't get rid of the dust. Some of them had razor nicks, which didn't heal as quickly as a farmer's razor nicks. That made them heroes in our childs' eyes. We stroked their nicks admiringly, I did too, even though the person I was allowed to stroke was only my foster father, not a real father whose cut would be stroked by his real child. I had half a father who told me to call him father, and would have liked to be a full father. That's why it wasn't difficult to stroke his cuts, and often I was made to feel like I was also the real child of a father.

Because our fathers could be called into work at any hour, it always felt like morning in Pfäffikon, even in the evening when the night shift arrived. The encroaching darkness was, we thought, a daily recurring mistake of nature, except on Sunday, which clearly did not know how to adhere to the law of timelessness. On Sunday, the station resembled an abandoned ship, and no amount of metallic whirring from the Verwo factory hall could dispel the silence. On Sundays, we couldn't be found at the station either. So, it didn't really exist.

The men from the upper part of the March district were different from those from the lower part. In the spring they absentmindedly chewed daisies and sorrel, and later glutinous grain or Joseph wheat, which they'd picked on the way to their home station. But they spat it out half-chewed, as if they didn't know that if you had enough grain you could chew it into gum. Then the sparrows arrived or the seagulls came over from the lake, fighting among the heavy shoes for the spoils.

In autumn we often saw dog rose branches between their lips. The men from lower March had only their extinguished cigarette butts from the day before to chew on, because their route to work did not lead through farmland and there was no grain growing along the roads, or daisies or sorrel, which people chewed in the spring. This is not a reason to assume that the upper Marchers weren't smokers. During the winter months they chewed on their unsightly cigarette butts just like their comrades from the lower village and did not care about their brown-stained teeth. They were simply people who lent a certain Sunday mood to the timelessness above the small Pfäffikon train station, which otherwise never would have existed throughout the year, since we didn't spend supposedly real Sundays in Pfäffikon and neither did the workers. We called those from upper March Sunday fathers, while the others, the lower Marchers, were called workday fathers because their route didn't lead through green farmland and so they couldn't chew on ears of corn or flowers or herbs. To be fully transparent, it should be noted here that my half-father had his worker's house built rather clumsily, and so a corner of the property stood on lower villager soil. I blamed this on our complicated family situation, on the fact of my having half a father to whom I would never be a whole child.

The fact of my having to call him father instead of foster father was never really something I held against him, as there were enough opportunities to take advantage of the verbal extension of a biological condition. When you stretched the first letter, it became a philosophical conundrum, because the *ffff* ...... emphasized with force, more or less negated the word's two syllables and led to a metaphysical realm where, with a little imagination, any biological condition could be denied or reinvented.

When imagination was no longer enough, I wished the half-father would stay completely in the corner of lower March, where I thought he belonged in such desolate moments.

Until King Haroy appeared and Josef Mächler lost his right pointer finger. With King Haroy, Sunday was introduced. Actual Sunday.

The night before, all the men washed themselves particularly thoroughly. The water in the tubs turned gray from the metal dust from the factory, where the tubs also came from. The workers' wives curled their hair and instructed the children to remove death's build-up from under their fingernails. Behind almost every kitchen window in the village, workers scraped beards off their faces, staring in disgust at their pasty skin that usually stayed hidden under the stubble. They were preparing themselves as if Christmas, Good Friday, and Easter were all happening on the same day, and all the saints were celebrating their birthdays on that day, too. And everyone talked about the upcoming Sunday spectacle as if they had already experienced it, spitting it out prematurely like the upper-March workers did their grain that never turned into chewing gum.

The village band played a march as the train pulled into Pfäffikon station, giving off a completely unfamiliar smell. On the freight car lay a dead monster that reeked of tar and fat and was called King Haroy or Mister Haroy, because it was a male whale. Its heart alone, announced a puffed-up dandy from the town on the other side of the lake, weighed five hundred kilos, which prompted our village to shout "hurrah" and "bravo," even though the dead king could no longer hear the ovations. People patted him on the back, stuck their heads into its large, gaping mouth, and shouted all sorts of things down its throat, until the dandy stirred again and announced more of King Haroy's dimensions.

Josef Mächler, called in to work at an unfortunate time, stared out the window. His gaze rested absently on the crowd, while his hands pushed sheet metal through the cutting machine. Then —a blood-curdling scream that everyone heard but wished they hadn't, except my foster father. He let go of my hand and rushed to the factory entrance. A short time later, we saw him with a swaying Mächler at his side. I felt nauseous and collapsed as a precaution. Before I closed my eyes, I saw my foster father waving his left hand frantically in front of the stationmaster's face, and gripping Mächler firmly in his right.

For many weeks after that, Josef Mächler was allowed to regale everyone with the story of his lost finger. He sat in the Sternen surrounded by the upper Marchers, his stump raised high whenever he cursed that Sunday.

King Haroy has been long forgotten. But Josef Mächler still curses, and Sunday comes every seventh day, as if the Pfäffikon station had become too full of itself.

italian migrant workers are doing construction next door

Italian migrant workers are doing construction on the Autobahn bridge next door. The smell of hot tar has driven the dogs into their kennels. Our square is empty and gray, except for the yellow car of the postman just passing by the trailers. Because he is afraid of the dogs, he distributes yellow slips in the mailboxes.

You have to go and pick up your package from the local post office. For Mrs. Tonini, this is quite difficult. She is old and her legs refuse to move anymore. So she has to ask her daughter, who lives in the trailer next to her, where geraniums are always in bloom. As if they could cope with the gray of the district heating system and the dirty yellow of the communal laundry. Color suffocates here. A mustard flower is blooming out of the top of the gravel pile by the fence. I am ashamed for it. Especially in rainy weather, when even the perpetually wandering cats disappear into the lower part of the trailers. Noldi has fashioned himself a green plastic roof, because it doesn't leak as badly, and roofing felt needs to be replaced every year. It's not like it used to be, when the older Yenish repaired their wagons over the winter. Now we, too, build for eternity. Anything provisional is laughed at.

People don't look forward to summer's arrival anymore; instead we have committed to an eternal winter. The children sing "The Gypsy Life is Merry" or "I-don't-know-what-that-means."

Even toys are different: domesticity in miniature farmhouse rooms, the inevitable Cadillac. The children come home from school in the afternoons. Standard middle-class fare is cooking on electric stoves. Hedgehogs and dog roasts are only mentioned in secret. Horse meat, too, since horses no longer pull our caravans. This should all be changed, but most people are too tired. Some are counting on the younger generations, but many doubt we'll even be around in the future, maybe as soon as fifty years from now. Will they taxidermy the last Yenish?

Only night knows our sorrow, night and the biting wind over the concrete. In the eyes of the old ones this looks like dying hope. I enjoy talking with them, for their silence speaks of old happinesses—flickering campfires and horses' thudding hooves.

Tiger moved to Switzerland three years ago. He'd been a horse trader in Alsace, and people say he was the best there was. Even a lame horse would hop like a hare if he'd decided to sell it. Tiger and his chewed tobacco pipe and his colorful, rolled-up shirts. Sometimes I hear him talking to the horses he sold, a low, deep song, red wine in his glass. Even his hat is old, his hat that he only ever takes off to scratch his head. He moves so gingerly, it's as if his feet were caressing the earth, the same earth that nourished his horses all those years. As if he knew there would be another going-back one day, which even the grayness couldn't prevent.

His dogs howl through the night, as the whores next door keep a lookout for clients and cover up license plates with their barely-covered behinds.

imparting wordless, empty spaciousness

imparting wordless, empty spaciousness. glass surrounds language again. emptiness, beyond my powers of expression, no-man's time, parasite in the middle of my body.

munching-munching-up-the-substance-munching-itself-full-full-full-munching ...

the arch of the body without soft tissues, iridescent green shell over the beetle's back. traces of burrowing left behind in the sands of time, escape. back. backbackbackbackback. sculling arms prevent the fall. the fall. a beetle fragment wants to live.

refrain:
a beetle fragment
wants to live
live
live
a
beetle fragment
wants to live
live
live
brain emptied of colors. black zone: kindly use straps. a beetle wants to learn to fly. to escape time and space and words hemmed in by glass.

Refrain:
a beetle fragment
. . . .
. . . .
. . . .
. . . .
. . . .

> Note:
> but in the meantime, it died on its own, the beetle fragment. it died. out.

i would like to leave this borderless white undescribed

I would like to leave this borderless white undescribed, but I've learned that emptiness can dangerously tip itself over, like a clown in a circus arena.

I'm not suffering, I've pasted a laugh into the crease of my seeing eye and painted over my blue mouth with a red that's unattainable (due to shortness of breath). It's the red of euphoria in early spring, the red of ... yes, Toulouse-red, peeled off and collected from vats of screaming happiness. A can-can in the shape of a heart, roaring tempo with an upturned nose, how nice it is that those condemned to hope are unteachable (unemptiable) ... I need to ... fear screams ... t-t-take ... take a leak ... but the latrine is missing a door handle.

On the outermost edge of the frame of a sequence of logical unintelligibility, time clings—single-minded as a salt-hungry goat and too short as always—hemmed in by distance, reflecting the trinity of all happening, what-was-what-is-what-will-be. And there time grins, and spirits smirk, visible only to the daydreamers, the unflappable crazy people. Siebenthal* tears are quietly shed, oozing into the mud of

---

* Siebenthal is a historical form of *Simmental*, a valley in Switzerland's Bernese Oberland named for the river Simme. This is also a common surname. —Tr.

long-forgotten non-conclusions; the burden of conclusiveness has now grown into a concrete living space.Harmless, therefore, this oozing—powerless.

Rage admits to the murder and slides across the polished wood of bourgeois righteousness. A Siebenthal tear dares to open its eyes ... go on, strike true, right in the black—use your fists if you need to, nail shut the rage and the horror. Living, or living dead—but not in-between.

As I allow myself the luxury of a word-mourning, a mourning savored in words, as I spell tears, and discomfort dances a sappy tango, bombs continue to be dropped on no-man's-lands, children are gassed, and mothers are shaved bald. The street you walk is always the same, and laced too tight.

Fists also turn gray prematurely, and rage, blind, now receives disability benefits.

it is screaming again

It is screaming again, albino-life in the process of dying. Screaming and mewling, animal and human, root system of the earth. Screaming, the fetuses behind white bars, naked vermin in stony nests. The shadows whine and plead. Sitting, Toad, amidst the dying with her eyes-eyes, otherwise nothing but face, babbles her madness into this screaming, and knives grow slowly out of her pores until they are big and cutting and black and cold with rage. Witches' voices throb in your head and smash your brain until it goes silent and the mothers the world-mothers push their fetuses into the trash cans of time. Plug your ears, you nobody, I, the turtle, plug your holes, your pores, smear your face and hands with blood to symbolize those without rights. You are white bars and fetus, are animal and human, are root systems and white bars, are albino-life in the process of dying. Are turtle, face, and eyes-eyes, are witches' babble, are stony nest and shadow and pleading, are naked vermin in an airless room, airless room, even you. Are brain, silence and scream, trash can, mother, and rage. Are knife, black from cold and from cutting open your wounds again and again and again ... until their killing finally scars on your neck and there is silence, silence. (Who wants to vomit up this filth at the bare feet of saints? Who wants to embrace this flesh, crippled and reeking of hatred, who wants to warm it, to clothe its freezing when it comes to it?) I wanted to hunt them on the back of the red unicorn, across all the seas of stone, through the tear-air and cauldrons of boiling blood ... yet I have remained a wish, one of theirs, a black pillar marking a grave on the beach where all of life ends, because one of the seven trolls is always stomping through the heartland, and morning always forgets the light. Until even the last word, the last syllable, the last scream, emptied of breath, finally dies—out. Night penetrates, deep, deep night. But no one sees those poisonous vapors, the encroaching exodus of hell. Oh, this weariness—of building dams, finally growing weary of strength, weary of fighting, of dying, weary of life, weary of guilt, weary of rage, weary of weariness.

the cell

No treachery! I cry and press my face to the crack in the door. If I could see myself, I'd see my three-part face and what the narrow strip of light is doing to it, I would see my face sliced into strips, two dark strips to either side, separated by a lighter one from the middle of my forehead to my chin—a precisely shaped, flaming tongue frozen on my face's center.

Because I can't scream and observe myself at the same time with my face pressed to the crack in the door, I decide to go on screaming, and so I scream *no treachery* down the hallway, with a few well-meaning warnings thrown in. When I'm finished I break into a hoarse bark, because of how much the screaming has strained my vocal cords. I bark and bark, I can't stop. It's a shame about the obscenities—I always save them for last, well aware that soon, they'll come bustling down the hall, lured by my cries as if by magic, and hurl my cell door open with *Nownow* or *Let'snotdothat* in their eyes; no, I'm not afraid of their injections anymore, or of that white cotton thing they sometimes tie around my back, or of the humane anesthetizing machine, as they call it; they haven't used that on me for a long time.

Finally hoarse, I try again with my obscenities. I start with the old woman whose house I burned down while she was still inside it. *I liked her!* I scream through the crack in the door—that usually always works, and if not, I follow it up with a flood of tears.

Nothing.

From there I move on to the dead siblings, and since there's no movement in the hall, I send the pathmaster Toni away with a howl. Still nothing. After further attempts, all I'm left with is mother. I almost suffocate on my sobs, I weep until my heart breaks.

Not a single footstep in the hall, no happy jingling of keys, no *nownow,* not even the slightest sound.

Damned cough, I sob desperately. Left alone; they have left me alone, I don't have anybody else. *It's not right*, I scream, not this eternity of silence in my cell, not this. What did I ever do to them?

came down to the valley, leaving now

(for Marianne Donatz)

She does it the way she needs to do it. She says she is leaving the valley. Broad hands beside the blue plate, her fork is in her left hand, the right rests calmly, not fluttering, almost an object itself. She has let herself take place. What is happening is happening. For several years, she has taken place in this village. At his side. She says she is leaving now. It, him. With this she looks openly at him, she searches his face, pokes around in his face, and he pokes around on his blue plate, somewhat bewildered. And speechless. He has stripped his rabbit leg down to its slender bone, the fibers of meat separated and arranged on the plate to form a crooked star. A meat star that has lost its shape, a star in the act of fleeing. He eats one fiber after another—fleeing flesh, one flight after another—unthinking, mute. He chews as, meanwhile, she explores his face with her clear, secret-less eyes. She says that she wants to leave, that she wants to leave before she needs to. She says this perhaps a bit too quickly. But he doesn't register this, it never occurred to him that she could leave him. In this valley, people don't leave one another. The only people who leave one another do so because they've died. He grew up in this valley. She says she will move to the valley's other side, that there is a steep path that leads there, to her. She is not lost to him, she says. Notdroppingoffthefaceoftheearth, she says. She is simply moving to another bed, to another end, at the other end of the valley. He refrains from asking if there is another man in the picture. He knows there is not another man in the picture. The star on his blue plate is disappearing. Now he has a proper meal on his plate again, all jumbled together, his plate looks the way it should look when a meal has been partially consumed. He feels the way he should feel. He feels the way he has on other days, after he's come inside her and is lying spread out within her, inside her wondrous flesh, always somewhat helpless and unfinished. He finishes the rest of the meat, which is no longer a star, no longer a fleeing star, and no longer a proper meal. Already, he is starting to remember. This is goodbye. She pushes her plate to the side, she hasn't touched her meal, just held her fork in her left hand, her right resting calmly on the table, a hand that's not like a fluttering bird, instead almost an object itself. He is thinking that he came inside her. Spread out, within her, peace assured to him. This is why she is leaving. She has had her fill of being a home. He is too at home in her flesh. Her affection is a burden. She wants to be something wild, a night-shadow creature, a monk, a lion plant. She does not want the voluntariness of things. She does not want these days of being taken for granted, days when he spreads himself out, inside of her, and takes from her flesh whatever seems beneficial to him. She would like to be invited to be flesh, would like to be able to decide, for or against the flesh. She hasn't touched her plate. She is standing in the kitchen now. Her sturdy body anchors her firmly in the dusk light flooding in through the window. She wants to leave. She takes place one last time in his life. He is so much younger than she, and this is a burden to him, his youth. There is no happiness in this age, knowing of the years she spent without him and before their time together. He is only okay inside her. His years go by inside her, not at her side. His love story is located in her flesh. He believes she wants revenge for this. He isn't a fighter. Her clear, secret-less eyes keep him from being so. Now he stands and moves into position in the room himself. A silent choreography. In the dusk light they dance themselves apart, in small, slow steps, silent. He wants to hold her back. She says once more that she is leaving. He thinks that there is no other place that he wants, because her flesh was his place and it is leaving with her along with everything else. She will leave nothing behind. He will not find the steep path, nor her house at the other end of the valley. He is not a fighter, and is ashamed because of it. His youthful face turns red, but he still stays silent. And still he feels, how she leaves, how she takes all of herself with her, leaving him standing in the dusk light, where he isn't anchored, as she always was. Dusk is her time, the time of night-shadow animals, of monks, of lion plants.

the souls of my sisters and brothers are singing in my dreams

No light, far and wide. The moon an unkept promise. A pinch of wind sifts through the cracks like a handful of ash that slips quickly through your fingers without leaving a memory behind to warm yourself by.

For a moment only. In the pause of a breath—a smile.

In minor, someone says calmly, the stars turn green once more, and a child is born who will write our names in the dust.

A burden, comes the reply. The person who dares to say it is sitting at the bottom of the cattle car, the same as the man hoping to see the stars turn green.

In minor, yes, says one woman with heavy hair and a faraway look in her eyes. Every other key has left us. We are the music of our wounds. Of our happiness and our laughter, of our death. She says this quietly, whispers it into the ear of the child resting against her breast, blind to the dark from hunger.

Cattle car, straw, urine, shit. A camp heated by heartbeats and leaps. Headed toward death, without the levity of their dances. Someone says, laughing, that you die the same way that you lived. On wheels, she says, and with a chuckle she sends her delusion into the stale air, as if she could use it to speed up the journey. Nobody sees that she is weeping over time. You try not to notice things in close quarters, to do so could be fatal.

As if light had always kept itself out of everything, they edge toward each other, skin to skin, pore to pore, as if light could still unfurl, a fire perhaps, and yet they know that it's only the straw beneath their body that's crackling, in the places where it hasn't been completely soaked through from sweat, and urine, and shit, and the women's blood.

As if to mock them, the violin stays tucked under the arm of one of their men. He is almost lost to exhaustion, but his fingers run up and down the strings. How quickly time forgets to riot when violin strings are touched and a few notes of music ask for indulgence. The eyes of the woman with the heavy hair look back from the greatest possible distance. Was that a bird that just touched the strings and freed the moon from the ashes? A bird, made lithe from flying, that broke through the belt of blood and crossed gaping ravines to reach this place? Just a wise lament, no trace of self-pity in the violin's voice, the player's fingers aren't sore yet. Who knows where the bow is, she thinks, and sees it silent, left behind. She's not asking for charity, just these notes, so her bare foot can tap to the beat on the straw, where the blood coagulates between the stalks and turns to stone when no one is singing. Residual tears flow from eyes and skin, cleansing, one note to the next, until the hand grows nimble, the one that belongs to the violin, and brings forth a song. The heart, harvested from curses, blossoms. Isn't every one of their songs both a lament and a blossoming at once? Even though death has already half-consumed her, has made itself at home in her bowels, rumbling, she still has her voice, so for the time being she can push aside the noise of all that is overwhelming the car's occupants. The unseen outside, deaf to the mirror-text of her stamping feet, forgets her and hums. It's not easy, stomping and humming. Both require space, something that never occurred to the men who beat them into the cattle car, laughing as women, men, and children fell on top of each other and crying broke out, because one of the children had been trampled to death. By the father, or maybe the mother, who knows.

The humming can still be heard even though the rattling of the carriage is drowning out the night. The voice, transparent as the garment of life, carves a path from one ear to the next, defying the muted mouths, wanting to connect them to her song, to her singing, which breaks from everything that was ever placed about their shoulders by mistake, burdening them since time immemorial. The interfaces of hope, her life, flayed as it's funneled down into dungeons where filth speaks in a foreign tongue, issue commands where there is no subject. Just a human, stripped down to the bone. She sings herself down there, inside, leaving flaps of skin, flesh, and intestines behind her, spinning one note around another, weaving a net she uses to capture the world, which she will always be.

And the night, says the voice, the first thing to be heard in the dark. She sings in a minor key like the morning had early that day, though we hadn't been allowed to finish greeting it, or live it out to the end. Only the stars seem to have forgotten us with their rich, forgiving minor key that we surrendered our bodies to as we danced. Suffering, on the other hand, which makes skillful use of our hearts and is different now than any suffering known before, mocks our ears by singing in a different key, in major, the key used to sing about emperors and kings.

The woman with a faraway look in her eyes twists her heavy hair into a crown as she dances. She still has a hairpin to fasten it with. "We are in the belly of the wolf," she sings, "with the stars." "E cara hamaske isi e bare chonutesa, pali, *korkorutne peren e farbe diveseske mamujal lendar."**

"It's true," she says when she reaches the end of the song. "Frost devoured the moon and we're sitting in the belly of the wolf while our colors, lost to us now, fall into the day."

"But not into our day, not anymore," she says. "On the murderers' day, they'll fall right into their lap."

We are driving east, toward a place where others accompany the sun and the moon to their death. No hope of light, it yellows in mounds of earth. Who knows what else is hidden underneath. This makes the crowned woman laugh. As if one of their own had stomped on the light at this hour. Everyone joins in, the dead child in their midst, as if this time were different than before: when they'd laughed over where they found themselves and direction didn't matter, east or west was all the same; they were simply pulled back and forth without a care, back when only a single ear of corn grew on the side of their path and one of them played for the women and sang and a deer dared to dart by, which they thanked God for with their songs. So it was unimportant then, east or west; they were on the road, and that was all that mattered.

In the eyes of the woman with the heavy hair, they now seem to be approaching a gathering place that promises certainty. They've ceased their singing. The woman lies down beside the dead child without ceremony. How quickly her face comes undone, for singing won't bring color to its cheeks and her feet can no longer keep time to the music. How quickly distance seizes hold when something is desired by heaven and eyes turn haplessly inward, to the place hope was still within reach.

So death arrives in minor, too, says another now, just like

---

* A Romani translation of the song's words. —Tr.

the life we gave ourselves to. Yes, says the woman, in minor. Life has already left her skin, and with one last jerk she tries and fails to push herself back up. So she lies silently beside the dead child, which could have been hers but could have been someone else's too, its face is no longer recognizable. Her dreams have been razed and can no longer maintain their place inside the woman's body. They howl for a moment before escaping her mouth. Should someone else step in and continue the singing? The woman's soul leaves behind its body and forces itself through the cracks of the cattle car in a panic, as if torture tools were waiting somewhere to make the death worse. The man who is still holding his violin and wondering about the reason for it all—there were so many whips, dogs, and guns, not to mention the eyes so fixated on them—he silences the instrument in his hand. In the quiet, the agony of hunger can be heard, it drowns out the rattling of the wagon, which, quieter now, is likely coming up on a train station or may have even arrived at its destination. Water, someone whispers, then he drinks his urine. Others have found their combs. They run them through their hair and try to do the same with the matted hair of the children, as if they sensed the rough craters growing under the scars on their skulls; there is the violent rebellion of brains that don't want to understand so retreat into trenches that do not permit entry to anyone. Every child for themselves, some shrouds to be found, which some greater knowing pressed into their hands. They try to establish a tentative connection with those combing them. A hopeless attempt amidst so much ash rain, which is plugging up their mouths, their eyes, their ears, and every pore, as if they were already flying on the horizon, disembodied, like a cloud that no sky wants to accept.

When the cattle car is finally opened, eighty women, men, and children tumble out. Some, because they don't manage quickly enough, are beaten out of the cell. Some of the dead are dragged by their arms and legs and hurled with a well-rehearsed swing into the roadside ditch. The survivors shield their eyes from the dazzling light they had longed for just moments ago. They will never be satisfied, murmurs one uniformed figure, wide-eyed. "Up, get up!" shouts another, this one laughing, rifle at the ready. "And sing, so that you'll enjoy the march." He slaps his thighs with a grin. Even someone like that can be made to sweat, thinks the man with the violin still in hand and whose torn shirt clings to his body. "Gelem, Gelem," he coaxes shyly from his violin, the song of the Roma, which tells the story of their people, and of the joy when a child is born to the world when a star turns green, who will write their names in the dust.

Oh, I was dreaming. A uniformed arm is resting on my shoulder. "You fell asleep standing up," says a female voice. "I was dreaming," I repeat myself, "maybe of you." "Standing up," the male one laughs. "ID please." Two different voices and two completely different sets of hands reach out to me demandingly. A man's and a woman's. Before I hurry to obey, I look into both their eyes. Completely ordinary eyes reflective of their duty. Bodies in green uniforms, pistols and batons at their sides. It is the 8th of September and we are in Berlin's Lustgarten, where "Never again" has been promised and celebrated since 1945. Laughter, music, and the happy cries of children can be heard. I look around and see my group again: relatives, friends, members of my people, the Roma. They're dancing, they're singing. "Gelem, Gelem" echoes from hundreds of throats, happy this time, not like in my dream. There's such hope in this singing, in the stomping dance steps of the women, in their elegant movements, which call to mind the many hands of the goddess Kali. "Any day now," says one of the officers. But again, I hear the two voices. Instead of finally presenting my ID, I say quietly, "I belong to the ones over there, the ones singing and dancing." No surprise on their faces, no reaction at all. So I take out the ID card that identifies me as Swiss. "We were only joking around," says the blonde woman with the bright blue eyes. "Although, they come in all different colors these days, and her eyes," she pauses thoughtfully, studying me, "yes, her eyes …"

A different arm around my shoulder. "In minor, only in a minor key," Rajko's voice, laughing. "Come, we've been missing you." "What are they doing here?" I ask, turning back to look at the uniforms and into the blue eyes of the woman. "Protecting you!" the woman calls cheerfully after us as we go off in search of our friends, hand in hand and with tears of laughter in our eyes. "Gelem, Gelem," and another woman takes me by the arm. "For the ones in the cattle car, for all of the dead, whom we can no longer accompany with our songs." She says this smiling.

We sing, and some cry, and we pile stones on top of each other, a memorial to our people driven through the landscape in trucks and cattle cars to their deaths. We dance in memory of them. "But in the future," says one of the boys, I think his name is Tschavo, "music will no longer be our only weapon." Born in the time after, life hasn't taught him how to laugh. His stone lands heavy onto the tower. Atop it I lay my crystal from the Swiss mountains, where long ago Gypsies hid from hunters and bloodhounds.

joseph sketch

It ran down his legs before he could unzip his fly. Oh, Joseph. Poor Joseph. He knew what was going to happen next. First this sweet warmth, which ran quickly down his legs. Then the unpleasant, nauseating cold. All of Joseph. Not a single human being to be found, and—human was something Joseph hadn't dared to call himself for a long time.

So, a not-human at the side of the road. One pocked with craters and strewn with debris, like the road itself. People had clearly made an island for Joseph, though it was impossible for anyone else to access. He stood, breathed, pissed alone. Thinking was unlikely. What was there to think about on a pissed-stained island inhabited only by Joseph? Who longed for nothing, who stood. Without an access point. Without any desires. Just the disgusting cold running down his legs, which he barely noticed anymore. I'm speaking in assumptions.

Joseph. Childlike smile. It runs warm down his legs. Part of his body is still suspended in his mother's womb. The poor woman, she doesn't know anything about it. Happy Joseph. The warmth. A rainbow arcs above his head, slowly, soothingly. A rainbow his mother doesn't see. Which no one sees, except for Joseph.

Joseph is crying. How is anyone supposed to know why they're crying? If they did, would they still shed a tear? Joseph cries as the now icy cold reaches his feet. Surrender, says the cold, says the ice. Surrender.

Joseph surrenders at the side of the road, surrounded by craters, on his island. He can still be molded. Into rock, perhaps? Into water surrounding his body?

Joseph at the side of the road on his island.

Me.

It screams, the ever-mute.

The island-mute.

Has anyone ever really seen him, heard him, or the clot of blood perhaps? The quiet moaning? The coughing after? And before? Just Joseph, all of Joseph.

Joseph: all of Joseph. Island-Joseph, Joseph, the island.

After every midnight, different days break, days strewn with seaweed and kelp. Light, star-strewn days, crater days. Everyday days, Joseph calls them, the days strewn with seaweed and kelp, the light, star-strewn days, crater days. Everyday-days, Joseph calls them.

Stayquietjoseph. Says the rock.

Worlds do not obey. Even Joseph's worlds. They happen like groundwater that rises to the surface without any geological knowledge. We obey, we've been drilled into doing so.

The Joseph-stone, which froze before I came to be, still weeps for the warmth of the valley.

always the same

Always the same. Ragged faces at a red-lit bar. Hands on dirty glasses. Hands on strangers' ankles. Eyes on uncovered breasts. Snatches of conversation. Smoke. Music.

Someone's laughing. An old man in a blonde wig with a signet ring on his pinky. His laugh is an old one. A laugh that knows lies and sorrow. A laugh to which love has never given a name. It hangs in the air without being fully accepted in its uselessness. Always the same. Everyone's laughter, long shattered against the wall of indifference. Buffoonery in a midnight bar, melodrama played out behind beer glasses. I order a beer.

A whore cries out. Beside her, a boy is puking between his legs. He's thrown out in a flurry of punches. Turned over to the streets. He'll find someone there. A rich man, perhaps. He will allow his body, defiled a thousand times, to be defiled again. By greedy hands that lack any trace of tenderness. For this, he'll receive a grade. Many do it for small change, others for free. And some are crying out for love. Always the same.

The band is playing sappy French songs. Phony, melancholic faces all around. Drunk, some, others quiet, lost in thought. A woman in a man's clothing flirts with the person next to her. Clearly a prostitute. Her hands tentatively stroke the young face of the other. A helpless gesture of affection, witnessed in a red-lit bar. They're both giggling. I see the prostitute's mouth flung open. She has bad teeth. They are both drinking champagne, they're both drunk. Her heavy prostitute-body sways on the red barstool. Her face looks pale and sickly. The same as every face in here. Maybe it's the lighting.

A young girl comes up to me. She says she wants a beer. A two-franc coin is lodged in her pack of cigarettes (brunettes). I'm not listening. I'm looking at her hands. Gruesome child hands, dirty nails. She probably works at a gas pump. I order two beers. She thanks me. I don't want to hear it. Many red-lit nights have made me mute and deaf. This bar's nakedness has left me naked myself. I feel all the sorrows of the world inside me, this illusory world. I want to talk about Brahms, or Beethoven, or a poem I once had to learn in school. I strike up a conversation with my beer glass, talk about Brahms and Beethoven and poetry. Poems learned by heart. The band takes a break. Someone offers me cheap white wine. I drink my beer.

I want to go to the bathroom. It's just been painted. It smells like paint, alcohol, and puke. There's a woman leaning against the wall, with black, empty eyes. She's on drugs, I think, and I want to get past her. Her breath smells like pills and alcohol. Empty eyes stare straight through me. Always the same. I have seen, experienced, too many eyes like these. Hands hold me back, and a face looms inches from my own. This woman must have been beautiful once. Her nostrils quiver, her mouth seems sensitive, so sensual. Only the eyes are empty — and gigantic. We don't speak. I think about the toilet and my warming beer.

Her lips seek out my mouth. Uncertain at first, then demanding. Her lips are hot and moist, her tongue rough, like a young dog's. A very lonely dog. She presses against my body in small, circular movements. I feel myself growing hot, I have to think about an animal again, the lonely animal inside me. Her longing penetrates my clothes. Her movements get faster. Then unfamiliar lips bite firmly down on mine. A barely audible sigh. Always the same. A body detaches from my own. Empty eyes staring at me. A sorrowful mouth begs silently for forgiveness. I take myself to the toilet. It smells like paint and puke. I think of my stuffed animals at home and cry. Always the same. It is everyone's crying.

snow-sister

Fifteen theories on the death of Swiss painter Esther Altorfer,* who used her body as the final and most uncompromising weapon against the functionality of submissive flesh and died under the wheels of a suburban Bernese train.

1. Snow-star then, or starry-snow: the word is clumsy, like the meaning of the aardwolf, a fixed desire, perhaps. Stars can hardly be called needy; they neither sow nor reap. They are placeless and genderless.

2. Her deeds mattered as little as her age. The only people who count either are shopkeepers, and sadly, our world is decaying into more and more of a peddler's den every day. There, even starlight is for sale, hawked by this light-fearing scum to that light-fearing scum—mischievous murderers, darkness dealers and light hoarders. What can be sold dies, incapacitated as a commodity.

---

* Esther Altorfer (1936–1988) was a Swiss artist who was active in the Bern art scene of the 1970s and 80s. She took part in numerous prominent group exhibitions and had close friendships with fellow artists Max Raetz and Meret Oppenheim—also deeply admired by Mehr—but despite this was regarded as somewhat of an outsider during her lifetime. Her work often drew from this experience, and also from her repeated stays in psychiatric institutions. These were likely strong points of identification for Mehr. Altorfer also used the pseudonyms "Jester" and "Schneeester" (Snow Esther). —Tr.

They used it to wipe their asses, they say, and filthy laughter rolls off their snouts to the sky.

3. Star Wars versus the poetry of space.

4. No one says to me, that star is black.

5. Your relentless poetry in every image, this strict, unsentimental expenditure, deadly suffering as a poetic work. At times, your brushstrokes are like laser beams, cold and unyielding.

6. Life as a barely sufficient determined existence, more of a coincidence, an abhorrent one, tied into, with effort, the laws of what is tolerable. Painting oneself beyond the edges of life, and then the certainty: endlessly wasted time.

7. Death as the most uncomfortable means of expression: this iron-crushed body as one final dogged painting—snow-blown Esther. The shopkeepers' seedy madness destroys even this message. Your decaying corpse will be haggled over on their checkout counters.

8. Is there a human attitude that would be more obscene, more vicious than the assertion that the quantities and possibilities of suffering are the erotic infinite—exhaustingly resolved only in the final, irreversible act of suicide? Then the stars would only be fool's gold, pyrite, Neapolitan junk—and agh, all that gaudy glitter in those croaking throats when in Capri the red sun sings itself into the sea.

9. Grim cheer in the snow-sister's eyes: the human race; this shameful sow, bestial like Michael, as if poetry were a dragon that needed to be deceitfully slain, one that waits for no death, but in life slices a sure and dreamlike line against the existence of functional larvae-beings. A passable line, a straight, drawn outside the edges, a final revolt against the exchangeability of flesh.

10. And keep fouling up the last pastures of pure anger, this bestial flesh of the shopkeepers, spoil the heaven that we created to function against all functionality of matter by breaking our words, by breaking into the baldness of their speakable stupidity.

11. Spoil heaven for yourself and grin under your skirts. There won't be an eye dry from greed when they make a mess of it all, these hammerers, these light-stealers, these starry-snow-officials.

12. And it's not my body, those bloody tatters of flesh at the end of the straight. It is the snow of a horrible innocence in the middle of summer.

13. Leadership in a state of war, graveside, the end of art as a happiness machine. Finally, revolt.

14. When we dance, the stars say to their gods, one of us falls out of the sweet security of the shopkeepers' souls. We don't give a damn about eternity.

15. When we dance, say the aardwolves, one of us catches the falling star in our snout. No one says, that star is black.

the checkerboard woman

She had to have known about her own particular, cornered sadness. She must have, I thought, as the embers in the fireplace cast a timid, pitiful glint upon her dull hair, gingerly, as a kind of final attempt. Desert burned in her round eyes. As I stared into her face, I had the sense I was a voyeur just discovering, and being frightened by, my own curiosity. She had on a white turtleneck. It was the only thing I ever saw her wear. Her dull, short-cropped black hair made a checkerboard together with the white. And then black jeans, too loose, always, and ugly, rusty brown shoes.

Bongiorno, she said, arms clasped wide around the corners of the table, and she gave a rigid, masculine curtsy. It was childish, it was ridiculous, it made no sense, and the smile that went with it got stuck somewhere, stayed folded up like a white, unused napkin. We ate *geisschäsli* and drank Barbera wine with mineral water, with grappa to follow. Alcohol ravaged my stomach, I felt slow. A sensual, masochistic feeling. I wanted to be as sad as she was. I wanted to look behind her sadness. But there was nothing to see there except that desert in her eyes and the pitiful glint on her dull hair when she sat down in front of the fire and allowed her narrow hands to rest on her knees, as if they were something foreign that she had to slowly grow accustomed to. Because we were being served by a drunken prostitute who actually wanted to be a photographer, or maybe it was the other way around, you never really know; at any rate—we only paid for half of what we drank. But she didn't seem to mind. It was finally the last day of the year, and it belonged to this folded-up napkin-smile. I don't think any of it made much of a difference to her. At the table next to us two men were shamelessly trying to flirt with the prostitute-photographer or photographer-prostitute, you couldn't tell which. Or with the checkerboard woman, as I called her. They slapped the skinny ass of one and laughed drunkenly into the emptiness of the other. Here an empty, meaningless giggle, there a tired smile, overshadowed by this damn loneliness. All giggles and smiles, the two must have hated each other, one lusting after the other for being her opposite, with one scornful of the other's isolation, the other of her helpless superficiality—and then the burning desert of the other. Here: cliché-level beauty pasted onto an aging body, a withered gray field worked by the hands of too many men, a feminine field, feminine to the point of becoming obscene, and there: an angular, boyish body, untouched, despite the two children this body must have given birth to.

I say must have—later I learned that she beat her children. The children had her same round eyes with a burning desert inside them. It must have been a desperate beating. Self-destructive, the cry of the fire. She didn't have any girls. She gave birth to two boys high above the crag between rusting garden tables, right beside the church dedicated to Saint Nicholas.

San Nicolao, they say there, humility in their voice. We always went to the church first. Two tender-looking Madonnas, one perhaps the slightest bit more beautiful, and then an early baroque tower and church interior like children wish for. Also, a huge holy water font where hands washed themselves endlessly in innocence; pious images of miracles some priest must have performed; the baroque crucifix; candleholders set invitingly in front of a Madonna. One candle cost fifty rappen, and above that, a Christian thank-you for our poor. A lot of marble from the area, likely the marble quarry. Yes, and over there could be where she gave birth to her boys, the checkerboard woman. Wine here, rosary there, a deceptive wine-bliss. She only beat her children when she was drunk.

what do they accuse us of?

What do they accuse us of? Our womanly ungratefulness, our moodiness, our trivial, stupid, childish outbursts. When we start to take ourselves seriously, they say we're vain. When we say yes when we would have liked to say no, they call us chatterboxes, and worse. I dream of saying no. I dream of rage, of hitting below the belt, I dream of what it would be like to Awaken and Know a happy moment in my being woman. I begin to deny these men the right to a place in my dreams, the same men who kiss my feet in order to crawl inside my cave. I start to forget that there are feminine words like giving and devotion and, in the process, I know that my shoulders brush against the icy barrier of our incomprehensibility. Because at night, dissatisfaction creeps over the bed and whimpers. Because the man lying next to me asks the same question every night: did I enjoy it, and I always say yes, the way I am supposed to. In the space where really, there's nothing to say. Because hatred grows in the loins of this obligation. Because those slogans the scouts say, like "Always prepared," make me sick. Because I have to desire the man daily to assure him of my love. Because I want to be left alone with my searching. Meanwhile my anger slams its fists on the table and bakes apricot cake and tea. I have to say yes when I think no. The no in the folds of my soul begins to rot and stink. Dear God, even you were invented by a man. And the women bowed down to you in love, offered their bodies with open holes, smiling blissfully in heavenly love. The house-husband is useless, and the kindergarten teacher, and the milkman is just a three-legged buffoon who wanders through women's fantasies. And in the end, we wind up at the male psychiatrist, who, with a grimacing toothpaste-face and his hands in his pockets, bandages us up once again for our being-woman. We forget our umbrella in the waiting room, which then takes on psychological significance and in housewife-speak means something like: I want to return to my helplessness, I want to crawl around on your male lap while you play around inside my vagina, for purely medical purposes of course, so that you can be sure of how capable I am.

böcklin on monte generoso

Böcklin on Monte Generoso. Fog clings to barren trees. An unknown mountain, cruel and sad. Snow slides quietly down its slopes and into the abyss, as if the mountain were a grave. They dynamited Hotel Kulm in the middle of winter, a hideous building. In its rooms tourists gushed over the beautiful Generoso landscape. But there weren't enough of them. And there was fog like they had never seen before on this mountain, painted by Böcklin. This mountain, this monstrosity. A ravenous, hollow-eyed beast. You had to look into the soul of the animal, there where blood-red holly berries slowly turn to stone. The shadows of houses are without contour, the road's edges unclear. In the branches, goblins— their cry is silence, is booming laughter. This, then, is the Winter Mountain. How she must have hated it. Fear in her fire-eyes. Sometimes, in December, yellow primroses bloom.

eyes

> Stasi says, almost spitefully:
> Then put on a pair of glasses!
> No, never, never again, Miranda
>   replies, it's no use, I can't bear it.
>   Would you wear them?
> Stasi counters:
> Me? Why me? My vision is decent.
> Decent, Miranda thinks, why decent?
> —from "Eyes to Wonder,"
>   Ingeborg Bachmann

But seeing, seeing with eyes-eyes. Wish, read off of eyes. Off of tree-eyes. Fruits, these wishes, surrendered to tenderness. Fruits of seeing, of perception.

Don't say, Miranda, or say it differently if you must. Talk about little brats and monsters. A funhouse mirror, distorting mirror of the soul, the eyes. Distorting gaze. In a distorted world.

Oh god, this misfortune. To pray it away, impossible, the real misfortune of misfortune. Miranda does not say. This, either.

Eyes grow their way inside of stories, into the trivial as well as the dramatic, into comedies and operas. Your gaze turns them all into tragedies.

You don't say it like that, Miranda, you just say that seeing turns into hell for you every day, seeing clearly. Living blind needs to be learned, Miranda.

Miranda, who does not say any of this. Sister with sibling-eyes. See-sister, that's the fever, and the fever is the eyes' rebellion. A rebellion, carried out with the respectability of a Tatar woman.

Miranda does not say this, either. It's impossible to season calamity.

Miranda, twenty years later. Sarajevo 1993. Death is the most uncomfortable means of expression. Seen through the decent vision of torturer-eyes, the bones in the woman's skull shatter, her brain oozes out. Her stomach ripped open, the child dies inside the dying body. One final blow with the rifle butt. One final look from the woman's eyes onto the torturer with the torturer-eyes. The muzzle is a rifle-eye on the splintering woman-eye. One shot and: see, Miranda, look. The betrayal of love follows its own laws. Today is no different from yesterday.

But then the lamb fields in the spring—beautiful, aren't they? Good fortune within reach as an expression of the joy of life.

Warsaw 1993. Miranda, Miranda. Under the bald man's expert gaze, a bloody Star of David appears around the woman's navel. Icy hands handle the butcher knife. The mob jeers seeing the dying woman. Eyes wide open, gaze plunging down to hell. Trying to cover mutilated breasts with bloody hands. She pukes bloody slime out of her torn-open mouth. Lays in her own shit and sees. Lays in her piss and sees. Lays in sewage and sees. Rats come scurrying from every direction and gnaw greedily on the woman's defenseless body. Eye-woman. See, Miranda, look, fix your gaze on the killing, on dying in sewage, the jeers and shouts now far away from that last look.

And yet, of course, the eye touches rose after rose, far from the wasteland of pain created by humans, the intoxicating scent infused with summer sun.

Solingen, Miranda, twenty years later. Running through flames, a woman with a child in her arms. Looks for a way out of the flaming hell. Whimpers, the child in the arms of the woman with the eyes on fire. With burning skin and hair. It can't see. It whimpers from pain and terror, the woman too, with the flames at her body, in her mouth and burned eyes. Watching, men in boots with a look that burns everything in its path, their work on the burning woman in the burning house with the charred child in her charred arms. Not a scream. Not from the inside out, not from the outside in. Look, Miranda, at the way betrayal pawns the love of this woman with a child off to hell.

And cries, the eye at the sight of the autumn child, for how could this be a child? Mossy green is the innocence on the ground of this young smile.

Mogadishu, Miranda, 1993. Stones fly, striking the woman's head, then chest, until they break. Jeering, the crowd, and the soldier whore barks fear from her body. Uncomprehending, the look of the woman, as long as she is still able to see. Because who wants to understand hell, no one, not this woman in the colorful scarves. Who hears the screaming of the mob, and realizes that not-understanding can be a revolt against the hail of stones. Strikes the eyes of the woman, the last stone, she is kneeling now, and pleading with the man whom the roaring mob has chosen as its leader.

Delhi, Miranda, 1993. Dogs paw at the body of the buried woman, devour the stoned woman's eyes.

Baghdad, 1993, Miranda. Sits, the woman in front of her canvas and sees. Sees the colors and shapes of her own personal fairy tale and laughs, cheered by seeing. Seeing,

Miranda, they laugh, seeing, these colors and shapes, and the way she sees them, this fairy tale deep inside her body. Then the detonation, Miranda, and swept away are the shapes and colors and happiness and laughter of this painting woman's insides. The missile, Miranda, in the split second of seeing, the shell—guided by the eye of the foreign soldier. Gashes a crater into the flesh of the earth, pulverizes the woman with the fleeting joy in her eyes. Dies, the joy in the woman's eyes, weeps, the child at the crater's edge, who knows nothing of betrayal, who will search for happiness, over and over and over again.

Zürich, 1993, Miranda, twenty years later. Jerked, the woman out of the car, Miranda, appraised with a hard look, assessed to be dirt and yet bored through, torn, and soaked with the murderer's seed. Woman-eyes seeing the look in the man-eyes. Seeing greed and black laughter and that biting and fleeing won't do anything. Bulging, her eyes from the strangler's strangling, the eyes bulge and rupture at the gaze of the strangler. No scream. The deadliest side of love, Miranda, the woman now laying huddled in the dirt like dirt, her tongue hanging from her mouth, her eyes bulging; before her eyes ruptured, she shat herself again, her ripped skirt, her bottom, and now the murderer's seed lazes down her legs, the legs of the woman's corpse unprotected from a stranger's gaze.

Detroit, Miranda, twenty years later. 1993. The woman hangs on the cross, rope cutting deep into flesh, feathered, tarred. Broken-winged bird, the woman. Tar on yellow skin, Miranda, tar and feathers sothatshelookslikeabird. A glance out of narrow eyes, out of foreign eyes into narrow foreign eyes. The butcher's dark happiness a happy sword-stroke through the eye. Miranda, Miranda, sister-eye, a tortured one. Is the measure of black love, Miranda. Hanging with the woman, the child. Bared, the teeth of the butcher. Laughs. Laughs, Miranda, and sees that she sees.

Vienna, Miranda, 1993. Runs through the hallway and screams, the woman. Is spotted, discovered, the woman. Is stabbed, the woman. Screaming, forget it, Miranda. See the man, see him, whom she has been with for years. Sees him, who sees and who sees that she sees, whom she has been with for years and slept with. Three crying children. Who see and hear and tell.

Miranda, Miranda, drunken happiness of growing blind. What is the virtue closest to love, you ask, and break, Miranda, sister-eye. Miranda, 1993. Your name like drifting autumn foliage. Moth-eye. Distorting mirror of love.

holzpferdchen's journey

Holzpferdchen, a small, brown wooden horse, climbed up to the moon and begged her to give his nicked, wooden body life. "Moon," he said, "give me skin, so that I can feel your softness, your velvet suppleness, give me a mouth that can laugh and cry, eyes that can see, give me a soul that can hear flowers growing and understand their smiles, give me a heart that can know the gentle rustling of the stars."

But Holzpferdchen could see that the moon was dying. Her otherwise peaceful eyes flickered darkly, and her mouth, which had kissed the sky a thousand times, was twisted in pain. Moon did not reply. Holzpferdchen sat down sadly, and then he began to freeze. He froze so horribly that ice flowers grew on his little wooden horse's body, and he shivered from fear and cold. Holzpferdchen could feel life; the fear and cold were giving him life, the same life that Moon did not wish to give him. Slowly, he left her. He gathered black stars with his delicate front hooves, crept back into the circle of cold, and laid the black stars gingerly on Moon's still chest. Holzpferdchen began to cry.

He stayed with the dead Moon for a long time. The cold wove an exquisite blue cloak around animal and celestial body together, a dangerous blue, latticed like the delicate spiderwebs of fear. The little wooden horse shivered and felt afraid. Slowly, he left the blue web of fear to look, to go on searching.

Holzpferdchen looked for the place people call sky, but all

he found was sorrow left behind by the dead Moon. A tiny planet paused in its path and wondered at this strange-looking celestial body, which was flying in spirals all alone, covered in ice flowers, freezing, scared, and sad. The little wooden horse was crying, and his tears turned to colorful glass marbles, which the planet children played with, an ancient game that the children of the earth play, too. And the big, blue marble of tears just grew and grew and grew.

Holzpferdchen went on searching, though he still did not know what he was actually searching for. He flew and stumbled between the stars, some charred and black, some so bright and hot that they almost set him on fire. Finally, just as he was about to stumble past it, he found the Tree.

The Tree loomed from one end of existence to the other, its roots sunk deep into the endless black of night, its crown towering high above, in the space where human longing gives birth to its own form and color, made perpetually anew, malleable. Holzpferdchen marveled at the Tree for a long time, delighting in the star flowers that played around the Tree's crown like a never-ending firework display, peering down at the roots to try and make out their end, he marveled and felt terribly small, tiny, a dot at the side of this world tree.

"World Tree," said Holzpferdchen. "Here I am, take me to you. You see, I was with the dying Moon, and before she died, the last shimmer of her golden hair caught between my hooves and her chest turned into a dead, silent plain. I picked black stars for her in order to take the loneliness of death from this plain, I stroked her quiet face with its wrinkles where her sorrowful mouth lay like the star flowers at midnight. I left her to continue searching. And it is for the sake of that search that I am here: I mean to search for life, real life, for love, and for forgiveness."

World Tree creaked—long and rhythmic—and Holzpferdchen heard a deep moan, like the dying cry of wounded prey. His heart pounded, fearful, as World Tree began to speak.

"Holzpferdchen, look at the length of my trunk, try to find the center point between crown and roots."

Holzpferdchen stumbled around the tree, his dark eyes fixed on its center. He suddenly grew frightened. There was sickness in the center, corroded, a festering wound in the shape of the little wooden horse.

"You see," said World Tree, "the place where you come from has destroyed my life force. I will die from this wound. Seven times a thousand years I have been sick now, and it is my time. The star flowers in my crown still twinkle, but my roots, Holzpferdchen, my roots are already dying and leaving the sky behind."

Holzpferdchen screamed and screamed and screamed. Pain and frustration made him unable to stop; he screamed so loud that the nicks in his little body began to glow and his dark eyes turned to black, glowing wells that threatened to consume the sky and everything in it with flames.

The dying World Tree fell silent, and Holzpferdchen could hear its quiet trembling, which seemed to be coming from deep inside its core. He saw the wound in the shape of himself, a hideous, festering wound that would never close again. And all at once Holzpferdchen understood the finality of everything that has ever come to be, both his own and that of the Heavens, the Moon, and the World Tree. The little wooden horse laid himself down inside the wound, he felt the sick, pounding heart of the World Tree, felt the shimmering heat that radiated sickness, felt the dying of the Tree in his own wooden body, felt the commonality of all pain and sank down inside it, he sank, and fell, and fell, fell deeper, fell down with the World Tree into death, slowly, as if dying were one final, intimate embrace between origin and end. Even the Sky collapsed over these final things. Black was the only thing the people on Earth could see—and the Earth opened itself up for the dying breaths of two beings with no homeland.

dorian dreamed

Dorian dreamed. He lay in one of the many white beds that the home, as it seemed to him, hoarded by the hundreds in hundreds of white rooms, put there to inspire fear with their hard, white bars. At least for Dorian they did. Sometimes he could hear the sleepy sigh of his neighbor, or a child screaming, and the stars glittering white and cold. Dorian's thirteen-year-old hands, square, brown little boy's hands, moved about restlessly. The dried edges of shed tears made craters on his hard, narrow face, and pain furrowed his skin—pain and sadness, fear.

Dorian's name was not actually Dorian, he just liked to change it, sometimes weekly, but often daily, too, and with a new name he became a different person, someone truly, completely new. This took away the thorns of sadness, thorns lodged so deep into his heart that Dorian imagined his heart to be perforated with holes of sadness. But now Dorian was Dorian and as Dorian, he dreamed. The dream had embedded itself in his interior moments ago, carefully explored his insides, and soothed the inner walls of the small human, dream hands gliding over the young one's pain, delicate as spiderwebs.

Dorian, alone and desperate for tenderness and warmth and security like all the children in the home, relaxed, slept, and with a small, almost fearful voice, greeted this dream that was very different from the others, from which he always awoke drenched in sweat and shaking, dreams whose powerful fists made him scream. Dorian's dream began to speak, quiet, cautious, so that it wouldn't frighten the boy: "Listen, Dorian, we are many dreams in this room, I am just one of many that have been sent here to comfort you. All the other children in these rooms will dream the same dream, and you, Dorian, need to listen to me closely now, so that you can feel and understand what I wish to say to you."

The ears in Dorian's insides listened attentively, eager to hear what this strange dream—which looked like a transparent landscape with fine, bright, round forms—had to say. And the dream—it was different from the dreams that came from Earth—continued: "We have traveled a long, long way to find you all. We passed millions of stars, meteorites, and even crossed paths with the sun. The sun is the guardian of the planet on which you live. She did not want to let us by. But when we told her about you and your companions, she grumbled something we couldn't make out and pulled in her burning rays to let us pass and continue in the direction of the Earth.

"Our mother is a planet millions of light years away from your own. Our mother was asleep until a short time ago, in a long, deep sleep. We dreams guarded her sleep, but then our mother awoke. She called all her dreams to the center of her heart. 'Listen,' she said, 'I have now slept seven times seven hundred years and seen so much, so, so much. Stars have combusted, suns have burned out, I have spoken to the great World Tree and followed the paths of my sisters and brothers, the planets.

"'I have seen a lot in these seven times seven hundred years, much of beauty, horror, I've watched new planets emerge and stars dance happily with one another, heard the quiet whispers in the World Tree's crown and the deep, calming hum of its roots. But I also saw ugly, horrible things—and evil. There is evil alive on Earth, a planet that you, dreams, have never seen or heard of. Evil is an animal that nests everywhere, it eats everything it sees; it's greedy, insatiable, and always on the lookout for new victims. When I saw the Earth, she was weeping.

"'Lux,' the Earth said to me, 'see these wounds humans have inflicted upon me, see my heart that they pierce again and again, see my skin, hideously scarred from so much pain, and see, Lux, how people are killing and torturing each other. I, the Earth, don't want to go on anymore. I can't go on anymore. I want to sleep your sleep, until my insides recover and my wounds heal over and my skin becomes as radiant as it was millions of years ago. Give me your sleep, Lux, you foreign planet, so that I might recover from this exhaustion.'

"Lux saw the Earth's misery, saw the festering wounds and the proliferating scars, saw the tears in the Earth's great ocean eyes, saw the weeping plants and roaring animals, but there too, Lux saw small humans blind with fear and pain, sleeping in ugly rooms with terrible, horrible dreams. Lux said to the Earth, 'I see that you're suffering, Earth. If I give you my sleep, you will recover. But tell me, Earth, who are these little ones who look like grown-up humans, but are somehow different?' The Earth answered, 'Those are the children. There are millions of children who are being tormented, beaten, bullied, starved, and murdered by war. And there are also my other children, the plants, the trees, the flowers big and small, the beautiful, exposed rocks, and all of the animals—insects, butterflies, lions, tigers, snakes.' Lux said to the Earth, 'Listen, if I give you my sleep, all of them will die, every one. I have a proposition for you. I will give you my seven-times-seven-hundred-year sleep, and you give me your small humans, your plants, your wild creatures, your insects and your butterflies. I will care for them and give them a home until you recover.' 'Very good,' said the Earth, but she was still skeptical. 'How can I give them to you when humans don't listen to me anymore, they don't speak my language anymore.' 'That is for me to worry about,' said Lux. 'I will send my dreams to the children, and to the non-domesticated animals, and your plants; my dreams will lead them on the long journey. I will build them a road of light, because my name is light and they will all arrive here safely.' The Earth gave thanks and started to grow excited about its great, long sleep. All of this the dream said to Dorian, and Dorian smiled a shy smile. Everything seemed so incredibly beautiful to him, including the voice of the dream, which came from another world.

"And now, Dorian," the dream continued. "Now you must get up and be on your way. Your planet, the Earth, is getting ready to sleep." Dorian stood up and pressed his little wooden horse with red wheels against his chest. It was the only thing he owned. "Don't be afraid, Dorian, you can take your little wooden horse with you, but you must leave everything else behind, for on your great journey, human belongings will only get in the way."

Dorian stood at the window, and beside him stood all the other children and his friends from the home, still fearful, and slightly alarmed, but beside each child stood a dream, smiling lovingly. And there, Dorian saw the road of light that would lead him directly to the planet of Lux. Tiny stars just bright enough to keep them from getting lost in the pitch darkness of night.

He climbed out the window first and began, with his little

wooden horse pressed tight against his chest, to walk. Now the others also dared to embark on the long, long journey themselves; they climbed carefully out of the windows, even short, fat Karl, always the butt of everyone's jokes, tripped over the sill and out the window, and Reto, who had only one leg because his mother hadn't been paying attention at the railroad crossing, hopped out on his one leg and even laughed a little as he did. They walked through the city and what they saw made their eyes grow wide with wonder. Children came out of every house, even babies, some who hadn't even been born yet and had a chance to know the Earth. The children came, millions of children, setting out for a new planet where there was no more pain or fear. Trees and bushes emerged out of the landscape, flowers, insects clung to the plants, and even grubs were allowed to come along and gnaw, as they do, at the roots of the garden vegetables. A long, long, procession, an exodus of all the despised and the outcasts. They came from every childrens' home, and from houses where big people with hard eyes lived. Some bigger humans were on the journey as well, but not very many. They had eyes like children and gentle, tender hands. And there was a dog, a very old dog who moaned and groaned, because the road was already proving somewhat difficult for him. A cat meowed beside the dog, and there were two guinea pigs, but all the other domesticated animals had to stay behind. But there were wild animals, lions, tigers, panthers, elephants, snakes, rabbits, and other big cats. They all moved so stealthily, and snarled (the ones that could snarl) cautiously, so they wouldn't frighten the plants and children. The few big humans matched the pace of the children, and no one yelled because everyone was at peace, for they all knew that now the hurt would stop, that wild gnawing at their hearts. Dorian walked and walked, eyes wide open. He wanted to see everything, this sea of stars, this road of lights. They passed the sun, who buzzed happily when she saw the great procession; they went past the moon, past Mars, past Jupiter; the sky was a single, fantastic kaleidoscope of colors and shapes. Dorian carried a smaller boy whose legs were too tired to make the long journey on their own. The large animals could see that the small humans were growing weary. "Listen," said the animals to each other, "we want to help them, humans don't have the endurance that we do and there is still a long way to go." And so the elephants lifted the children onto their backs, the most weary were allowed to ride on the backs of the panthers, tigers, and lions, the snails clung to the legs of the wild horses or the plants, and even the old, black dog with the oozing, tired eyes was given a spot on a zebra. The snakes twined around the necks of the giraffes, and on the oaks and other trees, birds chirped merrily and sang melodies.

Beside every child, every tree, every bush, every animal, and even the few adults with childrens' eyes, the dreams walked, too, humming to soothe them, so that no one would feel worried or afraid. It was a long, long journey. Meanwhile, Dorian had come to sit on a lion, the small, tired boy still in his arms. The little boy slept, and a dream guarded his sleep. The little wooden horse looked around in surprise, but in the end found nothing unusual about the new situation. The guinea pigs squeaked and found the whole thing very exciting, and the old, black dog had managed to fall asleep, too. He dreamed of a time when dogs could still roam free and were actually wolves, or at least lived like the wolves accompanying the long procession and howling here and there at a particularly bright star, because that was what they were accustomed to on Earth.

For a long, long time they wandered like this, no one really knew how long. They had forgotten Earth time, or their dreams had taken that knowledge from them. Slowly, any memory of Earth faded away, no one missed what they had left behind, the dreams had taken their memory of it all. Even their hurt dulled and grew quiet, and fear disappeared along with the agonizing holes they all knew so well. The closer they got to Lux, the more peace they felt in their hearts. They could see Lux now. She glowed a soft red and her warm rays reached invitingly to the long procession of tired earthlings. The sleeping children awoke, the animals began to run faster, and even the snails excitedly stretched their tiny heads with their delicate feelers out of their shells.

"So, here you are," said Lux. "Welcome to my planet. At last we can let the Earth sleep in peace." Dorian was the first to touch the ground of the planet. Carefully, he set his bare foot upon it, and with his toes he stroked the soft smoothness beneath him. He was overcome with joy. Then the others joined in, cautiously, filled with love, the littlest ones still timid. The trees and bushes buried their roots in the soil at once and immediately began to bloom, the animals dispersed among the trees and bushes, and the children and the few adults slept nestled in the soft fur of the animals, snuggled against their bodies, which were as warm as the belly of a very large mother. The old dog lay at the feet of a big human with light, knowing eyes. The dog sighed contentedly. There was silence on Lux, peace and security.

Lux looked around and saw that there was a stillness and order to everything. Then she turned her gaze back to the Earth and saw it was beginning to fall to sleep. Lux watched as everything crumbled to dust, she saw the desperate search for escape among those who had spent their entire lives doing nothing but tormenting others, she saw houses collapsing, and she watched as a furious wind carried away anything that might disturb the Earth in its sleep. The Earth was now bare and empty. But deep within her, a fire still burned softly, which after seven times seven hundred years would awaken again to a new and better life. The Earth slept, and it was a long, long time until her dreams were bright and light once more.

AFTERWORD

Zurich in the early 1970s. A young Mariella Mehr sits in a darkened pub, nursing a glass of wine. This is one of her haunts, an old *Beiz* that doesn't exist any longer, called Italiano. There is comfort to be found here, bodies and warmth and conversation, but despite this Mehr feels *mutterseelenallein*—as alone as a person could possibly be. A woman sits down at the next table over, and Mehr finds her so striking that, naturally, she has to say something. When she introduces herself, Mehr recognizes the name: Laure Wyss. She is well known in Swiss publishing circles, and Mehr knows her work and the journal that employs her. She starts to talk. She can't help herself. Wyss listens as Mehr tells about her childhood, and when she's finished, Wyss responds by saying the *Tages-Anzeiger* has been looking for a strong autobiographical, literary story. She would very much like to feature the one she's just heard. There's just one problem, she says, they go to press tomorrow. Mehr lies and tells her it's no problem, that she has a piece at home. The woman smiles and pulls her card from her purse. She tells her to bring it first thing in the morning and gives Mehr directions to her office.

Mehr rides the train home without a ticket (she can't afford one on her factory workers' wages), sits down at her typewriter and works through the night. The next morning she rides back into the city; in her hands is "Nightmare of the Embryos." It's accepted.

The product of that midnight flurry—what Mehr called "the first literary text of my life"—launched a career that spanned decades and roved prolifically across both genre and form. After that fateful encounter, Mehr was able to quit the factory and devote herself to writing—first through journalism but soon with novels, collections of poetry, criticism, plays, and short-form prose. "Nightmare of the Embryos," this collection's eponymous story, remains one of the most visceral and haunting pieces of Mehr's entire body of work; it is also one of the few that are explicitly autobiographical. In the essay, Mehr chronicles the horrors of a childhood spent as a ward of *Hilfswerk für die Kinder der Landstrasse,* or Charity for the Children of the Country Road, a forced assimilation campaign run by the state-funded child welfare organization "Pro Juventute." Instituted in 1926 as "the final solution to the vagrancy question" in Switzerland, the project targeted the country's itinerant communities, namely the Yenish and Sinti, with the goal of turning them into settled and "productive" members of society. The program was oriented around the belief that vagrancy was a hereditary condition, and that those affected were genetically degenerate, asocial, and morally inferior. To combat this "inherited disease," Pro Juventute social workers worked in cooperation with local, state, and cantonal authorities to separate children from their families, thereby severing the link between language, culture, and kin.

Both the Yenish and Sinti—distinct, traditionally nomadic ethnic minority groups—had already endured sanctioned persecution for centuries; it is possible for the Sinti to date their arrival in Europe from India to the 1400s, for instance, because of records documenting their forced removal. The Yenish endured a similar history, though their origins are more contested. Some sources claim they are a composite of various impoverished, marginalized groups that likely formed sometime around the Thirty Years' War. Others link them to the Helvetians, the Celtic tribe to which Switzerland's official designation (the Latin "Confoederatio Helvetica") pays tribute. Most Yenish contend that they are one of the peoples of the Roma, or simply "Roma," the ethnonym that replaced "Gypsy" officially in 1971 at the First World Romani Congress in London. This collective designation encompasses numerous ethnic minority groups that speak or spoke the Sanskrit-based, Indo-European *Romani* or one of its many dialects. This includes the Sinti, though many—particularly in Germany or German-speaking countries—insist upon an independent identity. There also continue to be those who identify as "Gypsy," just as there are many for whom the term carries a long history of pain and exclusion. These communities have also been variously referred to throughout history as vagrants, itinerants, travelers, and nomads. This translation has taken care to reflect Mehr's own choices, which means that "Gypsy" might be used alternatingly as a pejorative or an endearment, and that where "Yenish" and "Roma" appear in the text, it can be assumed that these were the terms used in Mehr's original German.

Even in a long chain of attempted erasure, Charity for the Children of the Country Road (1926–1973) stands out for its sweeping systematic approach, which was facilitated and backed by psychiatric, penal, and political institutions. Steering the program was Dr. Alfred Siegfried (1890–1972), a psychologist and former schoolteacher who served as director from its inception in 1926 until 1959. Siegfried's research on "vagrant children" drew heavily on an ideological framework put forth by psychiatrist and race theorist Robert

Ritter (1901–1951), who argued that vagrancy "posed a threat to the pure, German race." Another instrumental figure in Siegfried's conception of the program was Josef Jörger, then director of the Waldhaus psychiatric clinic in Chur, Switzerland, who championed ideas like mass experimentation. Ritter would go on to become the director of Germany's *Rassenhygienische und Bevölkerungsbiologische Forschungsstelle* (Research Institute for Racial Hygiene and Population Biology) in 1936. His genetic "research" informed policies enacted by S.S. chief Heinrich Himmler, serving as both tool and justification for the subsequent genocide of Europe's Roma and Sinti populations during the Third Reich. It is worth noting that while the Nazis' racial hygienic efforts stopped with the end of the war, Charity for the Children of the Country Road, which had preceded them, would continue for another twenty-eight years.

Over the course of the program's near-fifty years of operation, roughly six hundred Yenish children were taken from their families and placed in foster homes, orphanages, or correctional or educational institutions. Children had their names changed to prevent their families from locating them, and they were frequently subjected to forced labor as well as genetic and psychiatric experimentation. Yenish adults routinely underwent forced sterilization and castration. At the same time, church aid organizations, though technically operating independently from the official campaign, targeted Sinti youth using similar tactics to those employed by Pro Juventute. Official estimates today cite that, in total, roughly two thousand children were affected. Formal acknowledgment and restitution has been slow to arrive. In 1986, thirteen years after mounting public pressure led to the dismantling of Charity for the Children of the Country

Road, Pro Juventute officials held a press conference in which they issued a formal apology. Mehr, together with a group of other activists, crashed the event; no Yenish had been invited. In early 2024, multiple Yenish organizations including *Radgenossenschaft der Landstrasse* (Wheel Collective of the Country Road), of which Mehr had been a founding member, published an open letter calling on the Swiss government to recognize the event as a cultural genocide. Finally, in February 2025, the government responded by issuing an official acknowledgement stating that the tactics used against the country's Traveler communities qualified as Crimes Against Humanity, citing current international law.

Born to a Yenish mother in 1947, Mariella Mehr belonged to the second of three generations of her family to survive the abuses committed by Charity for the Children of the Country Road. Like her mother before her and her son after her, she was taken shortly after her birth to a hospital for "intellectually handicapped" infants in Zurich. At two, she was moved to a home run by Catholic nuns, where she lived for several years, leaving intermittently only for "treatments" (including the use of sensory deprivation tanks) for her "inherited intransigence." Electroshock treatments began when she was six. The rest of Mehr's youth was spent being moved between various mental institutions, reform schools, and foster homes, where she endured serial abuse. She has remarked that her childhood, if that is what it can be called, was a period "without ground beneath my feet."

Mehr seldom writes explicitly about what she or her family were made to endure—the effects are instead most often rendered thematically or explored in her use of language. Reading Mehr can be disorienting, induce discomfort, and at times verge on what feels like a violent assault on the senses. Her writing centers on the body and all its viscerality, and often privileges sensual impressions over semantic logic. The place she writes from has sharp and jagged edges—it is dark there, and the voice that calls out feels painfully far away. Mehr did not speak for much of her childhood: in an interview she recalls feeling unable to connect with other children in the homes, and shares a memory in which she sits crouched in a corner for hours, mute and desperately alone, with her arms wrapped around her knees. The impact of those early years left its mark. Isolation winds its way through this collection like a red thread, embroidering these pages with "invisible cages," with cold, white cells, and islands of loneliness. Glass surrounds so many things: people, tenderness, words. As she notes, "Longing screams wounds into her voice."

Books served as Mehr's primary form of connection growing up. "A motherless, wordless being," she says of herself, "I found mothers who had words for my confusion, for my inability to make sense of the world, for the often unbearable pain from the electroshocks and psychotropic drugs they forced on me." Writing allowed her to enter into community, to set her thinking in conversation with the minds that shaped her, and to locate herself within a lineage of other writers—particularly ones seeking to point to, cast off, or explode structures of violence and patriarchal hegemony within linguistic and literary frameworks, which led to their development of new and innovative modes of expression. "I can no longer remember exactly when it finally dawned on me that I needed to find my own language, my own words, for my life," she writes in her essay "The Beggar's Bowl." "I think it was after reading Celan's poetry." Ingeborg Bachmann was also foundational.

The piece "Eyes" opens with an epigraph from Bachmann's short story "Ihr glücklichen Augen" (Her happy eyes," or "Eyes to Wonder" in Mary Fran Gilbert's 1989 translation). In Bachmann's story, a very nearsighted narrator refuses to wear her glasses, believing her distorted vision to be a "gift from heaven" because it spares her having to face the painful realities of the world around her. In "Eyes," however, Mehr spares her protagonist Miranda nothing. Instead, she is commanded over and over again: "See, Miranda, look!" as she witnesses one brutal, heinous act of gendered violence after the next, each based on true events that took place in 1993. Readers are taken to Sarajevo during the Bosnian war, where a woman is being tortured to death, her skull crushed and her unborn baby ripped from her stomach; to Solingen, where a Turkish woman and her child have been set on fire by right-wing extremists; to stonings in Mogadishu and Delhi; to a domestic violence incident in Vienna; and on and on. The piece reads as a chronicle of violence against women written in Mehr's signature style, that is to say, in syntax that fractures alongside the women's bodies it depicts, and shifts to mimic the tunnel vision that sets in when the body feels itself in danger, reduced to the immediacy of a single moment's movements: "Whimpers, the child in the arms of the woman with the eyes on fire. With burning skin and hair. It can't see. It whimpers from pain and terror, the woman too, with flames at her body, in her mouth and burned eyes. Watching, men in boots with a look that burns everything in its path, their work on the burning woman in the burning house with the charred child in her charred arms." This piece is also a testament to just how entrenched Mehr was in the current of her times—just two months after "Eyes'" publication in the Swiss weekly newspaper *WoZ*, on December

20, 1993, the UN General Assembly passed the Declaration on the Elimination of Violence Against Women.

Mehr traces her politicization to age seventeen, when she was placed under "protective custody," or incarcerated for nineteen months in a women's prison without ever standing before a judge. She was pregnant at the time with her son Christian and claimed that Pro Juventute officials had put her in prison to stop her from marrying the father of her child, a Holocaust survivor of Jewish and Roma descent. The racial theories that informed Charity for the Children of the Country Road identified Yenish women as the ones responsible for passing down vagrancy, so measures were taken to prevent them from marrying within their culture. Instead, they were encouraged to marry into settled families. In Dr. Alfred Siegfried's view: "this usually put an end to the traveling, and thus, a branch breaks off the tree of the traveling clan ..."*

After her release in 1967, Mehr began immersing herself in research into Yenish and Roma history for the first time. Her people had endured a long history of persecution dating back to the sixteenth century, with the first record of a decree ordering "those without a country" to be placed on the rack and allowing "Gypsies" to be killed like game, with hunts organized throughout the Confederation. Mehr weaves these points into her stories as testimony: her writing is in many ways a memorial, a literary monument against forgetting. The more she read, the more she began to develop a nuanced understanding of the treatment of her people in relation to gender, particularly by Charity for the Children

---

* Dr. Alfred Siegfried, "Twenty Years of Social Service for the Children of the Country Road," Pro Juventute, 1947

of the Country Road. "It took me a long time," she recalled in one interview, "to realize that as Yenish women, we were persecuted and tormented not only for being Yenish, but also for being women. Only after realizing this did I begin to devote my political work more and more to the fate of women—no matter if they were Yenish or not." This commitment would go on to color her entire body of work.

Ultimately, Mehr devoted her writing career to the illumination of the shadows. Her early journalism exposed abuses of power and harmful disciplinary practices in various institutional contexts: she interviewed the "insane" in psychiatric hospitals and narrated from the streets, from inside orphanages, homeless shelters, and women's prisons. She was a champion for outsiders of all kinds, advocating on behalf of refugees, women, the Yenish and other Traveler communities. Fiction allowed for a turn inward, and the novel form, specifically, gave her the space for deeper and more sustained excavations into the psyche. Later novels lingered in troubled headspaces, featuring first-person female narrators who endured severe childhood trauma only to go on to commit heinous crimes themselves. (Mehr has remarked that her characters killed so that she didn't have to.) "The Cell" in this collection is an example of this—the fragment is a study for her 2002 novel *Angeklagt (Accused)*, part of a loose trilogy exploring systemic violence and female rage. Writing these works was emotionally taxing, but Mehr's life at the time stood thankfully in sharp relief to the books' darker themes: she was living in Lucignano at the beautiful Casa Rossa, where she kept chickens, cultivated flowers and herbs, and hosted friends for bacchanalian feasts in her garden. There was also space for her *Scharotl*, her caravan, which could be hitched up at a moment's notice. She lived there for almost twenty years, spurred by a traumatic, racist attack in 1997 to leave Switzerland behind her. The years in Italy were some of her best. She wrote poetry that spoke to a softer, tender side, and she courted happiness—a radical act that flew in the face of those who would have preferred to deny her the right to exist at all. As she put it, she belonged to the ones who continued to sing and to dance as the world burned down around them. *Gelem, Gelem.*

After being made to face some of the basest of conceivable horrors, Mehr crafted a life that was raucous, defiant, and loud with color. She lived in a house full of robbers in Pakistan, and in a cave in Afghanistan with a family she met while wandering through the desert. There she learned to milk sheep, and at night she slept on the ground with the families' thirteen children, their bodies arranged around the fire like a mandala. In 1983 she followed a friend to Spain—the friend was training to become a female bullfighter, and Mehr wanted to learn why women kill. But she soon found it all too horrifying, and so she reconciled the experience in what became an impassioned epistolary travelogue about sacred bulls, the divine feminine, and the lasting effects of Roman domination.

This volume is a testament to both Mehr's shadows and her joy, and her capacity to move between the furthest reaches of their poles. It showcases the breadth of Mehr's virtuosity and artistic vision. The collected prose spans various stages of Mehr's career, and is pieced together from anthologies, journals, and her personal archive in the Swiss National Library, which was compiled in 2015 thanks in large part to the care and dedication of literary scholars Nina Debrunner and Dr. Christa Baumberger. Some of these pieces were translated from the yellowed clippings of newspapers long out of print, others from typewritten fragments—musings and meditations—published here for the first time. Mehr was resistant to the corset of literary genre, and so the pieces slip fluidly between lyric personal essay, short story, prose poem, feminist tract, and all the spaces in between. Together they form a constellation, a kaleidoscope of shapes and voices and refracted light.

Susan Sontag wrote that "the earliest experience of art must have been that it was incantatory, magical; art was an instrument of ritual." These are some of the qualities most alive in Mehr's work—her configurations can feel atavistic and capable of stirring memories stored somewhere deep within our cells. She was comfortable in the quiet of pure sensation, having found refuge there as a child. I imagine that this was the world she returned to at the end of her life, as her diminishing sight sent her deeper and deeper into permanent darkness. The difference though was that this time, she was not alone—when she moved back to Switzerland in 2015, it was to a nursing home where she was lovingly cared for by her son Christian among others. In her final year Christian stayed by her side, and he made sure that she was buried in her leather jacket, as she had requested. Mariella Mehr passed away on September 5, 2022. She continued to write until the end.

"The spiral solidified into a fine net that wrapped itself around me, until I too could be absorbed into its ancient pattern, become part of its originality, which was feminine and earth."

CAROLINE FROH